ALSO BY L

Wolf Girl

Wolf Girl

Lost Girl

Alpha Girl

Mated Girl

Gilded City

House of Ash and Shadow

House of War and Bone

House of Light and Ether

Kings of Avalier

The Last Dragon King

The Broken Elf King

The Ruthless Fae King

The Forbidden Wolf King

Fallen Academy

Fallen Academy: Year One

Fallen Academy: Year Two

Fallen Academy: Year Three

Fallen Academy: Year Four

LEIA STONE

Bloom books

Published by Bloom Books, an imprint of Sourcebooks
P.O. Box 4410, Naperville, Illinois 60567-4410
(630) 961-3900
sourcebooks.com

Originally self-published by Leia Stone LLC in 2020.

Cataloging-in-Publication data is on file with the Library of Congress.

Printed and bound in the United States of America.
KP 10 9 8 7 6 5 4 3 2 1

To all the good guys.

TRIGGER WARNING

Themes of rape are present in this book. It is NOT graphic and does not get shown. It's a memory of the past and the word rape is used. Please be aware if that's a trigger for you.

CHAPTER ONE

MONDAYS.

I hated Mondays. They were like your period, they just snuck up on you out of nowhere and ruined your week.

I settled into first period with a literal troll breathing down the back of my neck. Starting my senior year in college with the same rejects who tormented me in middle and high school was not my ideal academic environment, but the only option available to me at the moment. Spinning in my seat, I glared the troll down. His nostrils flared, making the small tusks in his cheeks point upward, giving me a gnarly view of his tiny brain through his giant nostrils.

"Packard," I growled, "we've talked about personal space before. Please keep your acid breath to yourself."

A few of the other students snickered, but when

Packard took my bag and chucked it across the room, they quieted.

My bag hit the wall with a thud and slid to the ground, splaying its contents all over the floor.

Rage welled up inside of me as I closed my eyes, breathing deeply, trying to keep my wolf calm. Acid Breath knew what he was doing. If he could get me to awaken my wolf, even the tiniest bit, I'd be suspended. Even being cuffed at birth, my wolf still tried to break free every chance she got. It was something that was forbidden at Delphi High and was equally forbidden at Delphi University.

Breathe, breathe, breathe.

Fur rippled down the edges of my arms and I cursed to myself.

I felt Packard draw closer, the heat from his oily skin pressing in on me. "Go on, *Wolf Girl.* Show me what you're made of."

My eyes snapped open and they must have been yellow, because he reeled backward.

Wolf Girl.

Since I was five years old, the magical rejects that went to Delphi Elementary School had called me Wolf Girl. Why? Because no other wolves went here. I was the only one with a family stupid enough to get tossed out of Wolf City. There were tons of trolls, even more witches, a few vampires, and lots of fey, but the wolves… we kept a tight hold on our pack. You *really* had to fuck up to be cast out to live with the magical riffraff among the humans.

The cuffs on my wrists sent a magical pulse throughout my skin, and then an electrifying pain shot up my arms. Anything to keep my wolf at bay.

I hated this place. I *hated* what they did to me. The teacher hadn't entered the classroom yet, so technically if I could just calm down and not get caught with furry arms or yellow eyes...

"Take a breather," my one and only friend, Raven, whispered from her seat beside me.

Good idea. Sometimes she knew me better than I knew myself. Witches had a way with reading people's emotions.

I stood, tearing down the aisle and past where my bag lay splayed out on the floor. Bursting from the door of the classroom, I ran down the hallway. The entire time, my wolf was beating on my chest, begging to be let free.

Stay calm, stay calm, I told my inner wolf. She had a mind of her own, never listened to anything I told her, didn't care that we'd been cuffed and kept from shifting; she tried any chance she got to be free. It didn't matter that the cuffs electrocuted me when she tried to get out, it didn't matter that she'd never actually been let out and never would. She didn't care. The fur rippled down my arms as I envisioned tearing Packard's throat out and shoving it up his ass.

Just one shift, *one* run, one howl, and I could appease

her. Being human felt like a cage, and when I got angry it was even harder to keep her inside that cage.

My nails sharpened to points; the seams of my cutoff jean shorts swelled.

"Calm the *fuck* down," I growled at myself, my voice gruff with my wolf. Magic shot from the cuffs and pain laced along my spine again as I stumbled past a few witches.

Over a decade of being bullied at Delphi and my parents wondered why I had anger issues. Just once I wanted to let loose and show them all how much I hated them, but I was afraid I'd actually kill someone, and the cuffs would probably kill me before then.

I needed to release some of this tension, go for a run or something before I exploded. The last fifteen years of being this school's punching bag had finally broken me and I was ready to snap.

I ran down the hall, feeling the muscles in my body tighten and clench. The simple act of exercising worked wonders for taming my wolf. I did it often to ward off an attempted shift when I was around my human friends in my apartment building. One patch of fur here at Delphi with a bunch of magical kids wasn't so much a big deal as it was with the human population.

I burst free of the double doors and into the school parking lot. And that's when my wolf surged to the surface.

Tipping my head back, she let loose with a full-on

howl that ended as a human scream full of rage and agony. Pain that Packard couldn't be dealt with properly. Anger that I was stuck in this fuck-all of a school with a bunch of assholes who hated me, while my parents worked three human jobs to keep us fed. The cuffs shot out a powerful burst of magic and I gasped in pain, cutting my howl off from my throat as it turned into a strangled cry of pain. I collapsed to the ground, holding my arms as my claws retracted and the fur retreated. Nothing like getting tasered every time you tried to be yourself.

That's when a throat cleared behind me.

Oh. Shit.

My whole body stiffened as I stood on the tips of my Converse shoes, preparing myself to come face-to-face with a teacher.

Being a wolf, I was categorized as a "predator student." The only other species that got that designation here were the vampires, and the dark fey. The vampires were kept so well-fed no one really bothered policing them, and everyone was terrified of the dark fey so they didn't police them either. But me...if I partially shifted, growled, eyes went yellow, anything to show I was "threatening" a fellow student, it was all recorded and counted against me.

One more strike and I was out of here.

I inhaled as I spun around, and the first thing I smelled hit me right in the gut, sending warmth down my chest, trickling through my stomach and settling right between my legs.

Wolf.

Male.

Dominant.

Unmated.

One smell, that's all it took for me to know these four things.

"Having a bad day?" His voice was deep, husky, undeniably sexy.

My eyes went from the dark-wash jeans that clung to his muscular thighs up to the powder blue t-shirt he wore that was so tight it was like a second skin. It strained against his muscles, showing every dip and curve, even his nipples, which were pointed tight. When I got to his face, my heart jackknifed in my chest. Eyes the color of honey looked back at me from behind thick black lashes. They were threaded through with a deep blue the color of the ocean. He had a chiseled jaw and a chin butt. Honest to God, I'd always wanted to meet a guy in real life who had a chin butt. It was a weird fetish of mine.

Bucket list achieved.

"You could say that." I ran my fingers through my blond hair, taming any flyaways and trying to get my shit together.

Other than my mom and dad, I'd never met another wolf.

"You don't have much control over your wolf." His

comment probably wasn't meant to be cruel. By the tone of it, he was just making an observation, but it stung nonetheless.

I shrugged. "Why should I want to control her?"

His eyes went from warm honey to hot lava and I swallowed hard.

"New student?" I asked.

Please say yes.

Having another wolf at school would be amazing, especially *this* wolf.

Wolf Boy and Wolf Girl ride off into the sunset together and live happily ever after in banishment.

He shook his head slowly. "Just visiting."

Damn.

I peered out at the parking lot to see two huge dudes standing on either side of a black SUV that was pulled up to the curb. They had their hands out, stilled at their sides like they were going to pull a weapon on me for talking to this guy. He must work for the alpha and be here on business or something.

"From Werewolf City?" I pried.

I was slightly desperate to know everything about the place my parents were banished from.

His eyes slowly transformed from orange to yellow, and then to that striking bright blue as his wolf fully retreated. The blue of his eyes held a sorrow I couldn't place, a brokenness I felt in myself and recognized in him. It was just a flash and then it was gone. What could this perfect specimen possibly have experienced to be broken inside? This guy was insanely hot, movie-star hot. My wolf liked him immediately, but I was pretty sure she would like any decent looking male of her same species. We couldn't afford to be picky in a place like this.

He nodded slowly. "Why are you here?"

Shame burned my cheeks. I didn't answer, and dawning understanding lit up his face as his gaze fell to the cuffs on my wrists.

"Banished?" he asked, confused. I nodded and his lips turned into a frown. "Do they hurt much?" He pointed one meaty paw at my wrists and I chuckled.

"Only like I'm being burned alive."

A possessive growl ripped from his throat and I stumbled backward a few paces, not expecting it. He opened his mouth to speak, then the doors opened and the school administrator, Mr. Darkworth, stepped out. He was short for a fey, just a touch over six feet tall, and the wolf next to me had a few inches on him.

"Sawyer, I'm so sorry to keep you waiting."

Sawyer.

Why was that name familiar?

When Mr. Darkworth saw me there, he looked startled. "Demi, I trust you are behaving?" He glared down his nose at me.

I tucked a chunk of long blond hair behind my ear and nodded. "Just getting…a bit of fresh air, sir."

I moved to go back inside, taking this as my cue

to bolt, when Sawyer's hand snaked out and grabbed me gently by the upper arm. My heart jumped into my throat at his touch, his eyes blazing yellow as I looked up at him.

"Do you like it here?" His voice was gruff, his wolf close.

I snort-laughed. "Are you serious?"

How could I be happy here? As a wolf I needed to live among my kind or I'd go wild. Thank God for Mom and Dad or I would have to be put down. *No one* liked living here, on the outskirts of Magic City, crammed in with the humans. It was awful.

He released my arm, blinked twice, eyes flashing from yellow back to blue as if shaking off his wolf.

Mr. Darkworth frowned. "Shall we, son?" He motioned Sawyer into the double doors that led to his office, and I took the other set back to class.

When I sat down, I noticed Raven had gathered up the contents of my book bag and placed it on my seat. I gave her a smile of thanks and then spent the rest of the class staring at a spot on the wall and wondering what the hell just happened and who that guy Sawyer was.

The next few hours, Sawyer filled my every thought. He saw me lose my shit and howl. How embarrassing...and he was here "visiting." That was vague as fuck. I told Raven about it at lunch and she was all ears.

"How old was he?" She leaned forward, twirling a blue chunk of hair between her fingers.

I shrugged. "Same age as me? Twenty-one. Maybe twenty-two?"

"Want me to do a spell and find out why he was here?" Her eyes glittered and I grinned.

"Nah, I like the mystery," I said. "I'll brew on it for years, wondering where the man of my dreams went before I settle down and marry a human."

Raven snickered. "You sure?" She motioned over to Isaacs's table. "He'd take you back in a heartbeat."

I clamped a hand over her mouth. "We *do not* speak of the time I hooked up with a fey, okay?" Peeling my fingers from her mouth one by one, she laughed.

"You said you liked it," she reminded me.

I pulled a chicken tender from my plate and pointed it at her throat. "Speak another word of this and die."

Isaac was hot, but he had a weird foot fetish thing, and I wasn't feeling the pointy ears. It was a phase and Raven knew that.

"Maybe he's on socials. Sawyer, any last name?" Raven pulled out her phone, ready to detective the fuck out of this guy.

"Nope. Just Sawyer." I peered over her shoulder as she typed Sawyer into Instagram and started to scroll through profiles. We were about halfway down the page when the cafeteria doors burst open. Four hulking males fanned out and scanned the crowd, and one female with bright red hair brought up the rear.

I didn't need to smell them to know they were werewolves. I could see it in their stances, the way they sniffed the air and searched the cafeteria with yellow eyes.

Oh shit.

What did I do? I shrank in my seat, trying to disappear, when one of them looked directly at me. A quick scan told me none of them were Sawyer.

Maybe he went back and asked the alpha about a girl named Demi who was cast out of the pack, and they said I shouldn't be allowed to go to school here, or maybe—

"Demi Calloway?"

I held my breath as terror rushed through me. "Yes?" I squeaked.

The dude hovering over me was jacked, a huge wolf, who I now recognized as one of the guys waiting by the car this morning in the school parking lot. There was a gun at his hip, likely filled with silver bullets, and a vampire stake in a holster at his thigh. This dude wasn't messing around.

He handed me a letter with a golden wax seal. Legit it had a wax seal like this was 1601.

I gulped, taking the letter. "Thanks." I attempted to shove it in my bag and prayed he'd go away.

"Open it," the wolf growled.

Crap.

The whole cafeteria was watching me now. Even the lunch lady looked nervous for me.

Tearing the seal, bits of gold wax falling into my lap, I rolled the letter open and scanned it. Typed in an italic font was a letter addressed to me.

Demi Calloway,

You are hereby cordially invited to attend Sterling Hill Collegiate Academy of Werewolf Sciences. Werewolf Law 301.6 states that all unmated females ages 18–22 must be present the year the future alpha chooses his mate.

Sincerely,
Werewolf City alpha in residence, Curt Hudson

What the what! My heart hammered in my chest as I noticed a personal note at the bottom scrawled in messy handwriting.

P.S. This was the only way I could legally get you out of there.

Sawyer Hudson.

My stomach dropped, my mouth going dry.

Sawyer Hudson.

Sawyer.

Hudson.

Curt Hudson was alpha of Werewolf City, which meant…Sawyer was the *fucking* alpha's son. I'd met the alpha's son and now I was being invited back to Werewolf City because he was choosing a mate? What in the actual hell was happening?

I stared at the sheet of paper in my hand and then looked up at the dude. "Uhh, cool, thanks. I'll…think about it."

He shook his head. "I was told by the alpha to tell you the offer expires in sixty seconds. He does not hold your parents' transgressions upon you. But he wants to deal with this matter quickly."

Whoa. Sixty seconds? He didn't hold my parents' transgressions against me? What did that mean? That despite their banishment, I was being given a place back into werewolf society? I had to chew the inside of my lip to bite back the tears. I stared at the cuffs on my wrist, letting my mind process his words.

"Those will come off. You'll be a regular member of society with proper living accommodations and a clean slate." The guard seemed to be reading off of a second paper that he held. "You have thirty seconds."

Raven flew into my arms, pulling me into a hug, and the entire cafeteria went silent as they watched me decide. "Go," Raven whispered in my ear. "I'll tell your parents. They would want this for you."

My parents. I couldn't just leave them. Could I?

She pulled away from me and I looked up at the dude. "Can I pick up my stuff? See my parents?"

He shook his head, crossing his arms over his chest. "You'll be given new things. Your parents are not permitted to know about this until after you arrive in Werewolf City."

A sob formed in my throat, but I pushed it down. I couldn't let these fuckers see my weakness.

Go to Sterling Hill? Live among werewolves again? It's *all* I'd wanted since I was a little girl. I had no idea why my parents were banished from Werewolf City; they never spoke about it. Said it wasn't for children's ears, and then when I became a teenager, my father told me it was too painful. I figured it didn't really matter anyway. What was done was done, lifelong banishment to the reject pile of the city, destined to live among magical trash and humans for the rest of my life. Delphi Corner was a small five-square-mile area in Spokane, Washington, which was spelled to repel humans, so we could be ourselves here, but if we stepped outside the area, we needed to be on our best behavior and appear human...assuming that was possible.

I glanced at Packard. He'd probably never been outside Delphi Corner. Not like I had, or the vampires or witches. Since we could easily appear human, we were allowed to get human jobs and live and shop among them.

"Time's up." His voice was sharp and I knew he wouldn't wait a second longer.

Leave Delphi? Leave my parents? Go back to Werewolf City... All because I'd met the alpha's son for five seconds and he was picking his mate this year?

It was...wild.

A dream come true?

I looked again at the cuffs on my wrists. To be able to shift, to finally let my wolf out...I couldn't conceive of it. She shook my skin like it was a cage and in that moment my decision was made for me.

"I accept." I stood, my voice husky from my wolf's rise to the surface. The guard nodded and indicated I follow him. I looked down at Raven and her wide-eyed expression. Tears pooled in her gaze.

"I'll call you tonight," I whispered as I leaned down and gave her a final hug.

"This is wild, but I love you," she whispered, and my throat tightened.

"Holy fucking shit I love you back," I half sobbed.

Standing, I brushed my eyes clear of any emotion, and followed the beefy wolves to the double doors.

I was finally leaving this hellhole. I thought that they would let me go in peace, but then I felt a wet thud to the back of my head and I knew that just wasn't true. It didn't hurt so much as it startled me. Something wet ran down my neck, and with a plop, an orange slice fell to the ground.

"Later, *Wolf Girl*!" It was Bianca. I would know that shrill nasally voice anywhere. Fucking Bianca. That dark fey had the heart of a devil.

Fur rippled down my arms and then the cuffs lit up, electrocuting me, bringing me to my knees in pain. Laughs filled the cafeteria and I just wanted to die. It was their favorite thing to do, laugh while I was shocked to shit. All of the wolves who'd come to escort me looked at me with pity. I was so freaking embarrassed. When you're bullied for so many years, a few things can happen:

1. You can become really shy and introverted, sink into yourself and want to disappear.
2. You become a bully yourself, angry and mad at the world.
3. You get numb to it after a while, so dead inside emotionally it doesn't really bother you anymore. It's like you expect it.

I was somewhere between two and three. Angry but numb to it all. Over the course of my education here I'd been called a dog, told I smelled like shit, been given flea shampoo, and for prom, someone hung a rhinestone collar and leash on my locker. I just didn't care anymore.

"Let's just go," I told the wolf guards as I stood, shaking off the incident, because they were looking at me like they were waiting for me to wolf out and rip

Bianca's head off. I wanted to, I did, but I wanted to leave this place forever more.

One of the wolf guards who'd come with them, the tall female with red hair, reached out to a passing witch and grabbed the apple off her tray. Then she reeled her arm back and chucked it. I followed the red apple, surprised at the sudden throw, and grinned as it knocked into the side of Bianca's head.

Every student in the place stood then and the lead guard shot the redheaded wolf a glare. "Let's go before they curse us."

"Worth it." The redhead winked at me.

Emotion clogged my throat. My entire life I'd been alone, a freak, a wolf without a pack, no one but Raven to count on, and now...

My happy emotions were short-lived. A black bag was thrown over my head, plunging me into darkness.

"Sorry, kiddo, the alpha gave strict instructions not to trust you with the location of the school just yet."

A firm arm gripped me under my armpit and I was marched forward blindly.

By the time we got outside and I heard a van door roll open, I found myself wondering what the hell had just happened.

Mondays.

CHAPTER TWO

WE LISTENED TO VAN HALEN THE ENTIRE DRIVE. Like an *entire* album. It was at least an hour before the van slowed to a crawl. No one said much to me the entire time except to ask if I needed to pee or have water. I felt like a prisoner but not; it was weird. My hands weren't tied, I was just told to keep this bag loosely over my head the whole drive, which was triggering some serious PTSD. I didn't like being in small spaces.

The alpha obviously didn't trust me, which made me wonder how hard Sawyer had to beg him to let me back into Werewolf City. Why would Sawyer do that? I'd met him all of two minutes. Granted, it was an intense meeting, but I didn't think I'd impressed him with my angry outburst and shabby clothes.

"So, like, can we really not date any girls this year until Sawyer picks his mate?" one of the males asked, turning down the music. My whole body tensed as I leaned into the conversation, curious what the answer would be.

Another dude chuckled. "Nah, he'll pick his top twenty pretty quickly and then you just stay away from them."

What the hell? Twenty girls to date all year?

What was this, *Werewolf Bachelor*?

"Sophia Green is so hot. I've wanted her since first grade. He better not pick her," a third male said.

There was a smacking sound and then a groan. "Women are not objects, you fools," the redheaded female chided them. "The girl Sawyer ends up with will have to choose him just as much as he chooses her."

Collective laughter rocked through the car. "And what female at school *wouldn't* pick pretty boy Sawyer?"

"I wouldn't," the female said.

Silence.

"You're his cousin. Gross," a male voice commented.

"*So?* I wouldn't pick him. Now stop talking about the mating year, it's making me nauseous. I have to live with it for the next year," she snapped back.

Cousin? She was Sawyer's cousin?

We rode in silence a few more minutes until the van stopped.

"We're here. I'm taking the cover off of her head," the female said.

"Copy that," a male answered.

Finally!

When the bag was ripped off my head, I was blinded with bright light. I winced as my eyes adjusted to the sudden sunlight assaulting my brain.

"Hey, Brandon," someone outside of the car said.

I swiveled my head in that direction to see a guard standing in front of a giant iron gate. He wore black army fatigues with a gun at his hip. "That her?" He peered inside of the car at me.

What the...?

He looked me up and down, causing redness to creep up my neck. "Now I see why Sawyer went to all that trouble."

"She can hear you, asshole!" Redhead snapped.

The guard rapped a palm on the hood of the van twice and we rolled forward into the open gates.

Holy shifter babies.

My jaw unhinged as we passed a low stone wall with the name *Sterling Hill University* on it. It wasn't the letters that had me transfixed, it was the freaking building and manicured lawns. The campus was sprawled out onto a wide green lawn, with several buildings made of glass and stainless steel. Everything was so modern. Students walked on the sidewalks, but a few wolves lay on the lawns, sunbathing in their animal form.

I gasped and Redhead looked at me, following my gaze.

She frowned, then looked at the cuffs on my wrists. "When's the last time you shifted?"

It was an innocent question, one I'm sure she didn't think would carry so much pain.

"Never." My voice cracked. "I was born outside Werewolf City," I told her.

"Jesus," the driver dude said.

"Language," the guy in the passenger seat growled.

The driver flipped him off and the dude in the passenger seat grabbed the finger and bent it backward until the driver conceded. "Okay, okay, I'm sorry, baby Jesus."

"That's better," passenger guy said, and when I looked at the redheaded chick again, she was smiling.

I was grateful for the distraction.

"I'm Sage," she told me, holding out a hand.

Sage. That was an interesting name.

"My mom's a hippie." She winked and I took her hand.

I shook it. "Demi."

She gestured over her shoulder to the driver, "That's Brandon, total player and asshole. Stay *away* from him."

"Hey!" he yelled.

She motioned to the guy in the passenger seat. "And that's Quan. Sweet teddy bear, you can trust him with your life."

"Love you, Sage."

"Love you too, boo," she called back.

There was a guy sitting next to Sage who was silently staring out the window. "That's Walsh, he's basically a mute."

"Fuck you," he growled, causing her to grin.

"But if I had to pick one guy to have my back in a fight, it would be him."

"Hey!" the driver, Brandon, yelled again.

"Sorry, babe, you're worthless. Nothing but eye candy." Sage shrugged, then looked at me, winking as Brandon started to pout.

"I can't help that I'm so beautiful," Brandon declared.

Everyone chuckled, including me.

I liked her, I liked all of them, even though this was the weirdest fucking day of my life.

We pulled into a parking spot, in between a Range Rover and a BMW, and I started to second guess my decision to come here. My jean shorts were torn, with heavily frayed edges, and my Converse shoes that I'd snagged at a second-hand store had duct tape on the bottom to keep the sole from coming off. Not to mention my t-shirt was vintage and looked like I'd pulled it out of a trash can. I'd had it custom screen printed with *Coffee before talkie* across the front.

I clearly didn't belong here.

Brandon killed the engine and opened the sliding van door, rolling out his neck. "I'll take her to admissions, then she's no longer our problem."

Ouch. I take it back, I didn't like *all* of them.

"You're a dick, you know that? *I'll* take her." Sage jumped out of the van and he was forced to back up or she'd plow right into him.

He just rolled his eyes and waved her off. “Whatever.”

The other boys jumped out of the van as well and looked at me. “I hope you like it here. It was nice to meet you,” Quan said, taking off his belt which held two guns. I noticed a large gold cross hung from his neck.

“Thanks...” I cleared my throat, “for the kidnapping.”

Sage grinned, and even Walsh’s lips twitched like he wanted to smile.

“She’s funny. I like her,” Sage told Quan, then she grabbed me by the arm and dragged me away from the van. I followed her, suddenly conscious of the wrist cuffs that *no one else* had. People stared as we passed, but when they did, Sage flipped them off so they quickly turned their heads.

“Big news on campus. The alpha’s son goes to meet with the principal of the magical rejects for charity work and is so taken with a banished wolf that he begs his father to free her and let her back into the city so she can be considered as a potential mate for his mating year. Quite romantic, if you like that shit.”

“No. No. It’s not like that,” I told her, my cheeks reddening. “He just used the mate choosing thing as a way to get me out. He even said so in his letter.”

My cheeks pinked again just thinking about it as we passed another group of people who stared. I tucked my chin into my chest and looked at the ground, wanting to disappear. I didn't like attention. I liked life better through the lens of my camera.

Sage's hand rose and jerked my chin up as she stopped walking and leaned into my ear. "Honey, you're a wolf. Looking down when stared at is just going to get your ass kicked."

I gulped.

This was *so* different from Delphi Academy.

I nodded.

"Submissives don't go to Sterling Hill, and I can smell your dominance, so just let it out, okay?"

Let it out? The one thing I'd shoved deep down inside of me my entire life?

"Got it," I said, my voice stronger. "Anything else?"

This chick seemed knowledgeable, and since my parents never spoke much of Werewolf City or their time at Sterling Hill because of the pain it brought them, I knew shit-all about this place, or how to survive here. I'd never shifted, never lived in a pack. I grew up with a bunch of stuck-up magical assholes as a solitary wolf girl. Everyone at that school was a grade-A asshole except for Raven. Without her, I might not have survived it.

Sage nodded, hissing like a cat at a passing girl, who scurried away, leaving Sage grinning. When she was done, she leaned back in to face me. "Every female at this school wants to marry my cousin Sawyer and be the alpha's wife, and every single one now knows that he brought you here to join the dating pool. *Watch* your back."

Then she turned and walked off, leaving me speechless and with a lump in my throat.

Join the dating pool? Holy shit, I really *was* in *Werewolf Bachelor*.

"Come on!" she snapped, and I ran after her, throwing some glares of my own as I passed. Every female here was dressed like a doll. Full-on high heels, dresses, slacks and silk shirts. Hair was curled and set in place and makeup was on-point. Not an eyebrow hair out of place. Meanwhile, I looked like I'd rolled out of bed and threw on whatever was closest and smelled generally clean, which wasn't far from the truth.

I ran after Sage and followed her around a corner to a giant glass dome building marked *Admissions*.

She stopped at the door and faced me. "I'm a junior. I live in Lexington Hall. Suite Eleven. Try to get on my floor and I'll take you under my wing."

My heart pinched at her generosity and I nodded. "Thanks, girl." I looked down at her chin out of habit and she inclined her head, smoothing her bright red hair over one shoulder and tipping my chin up to meet her eyes.

"Remember, give 'em hell. You're one of us now."

With that, she turned and walked away, leaving me to stand in front of the double glass doors.

You're one of us now. She had no way of knowing how much that meant to me.

Okay...here goes nothing.

Reaching out, I pulled the doors open and stepped inside.

Whoa.

The dome ceiling was tinted, but it still let shafts of light in, and behind it was all forest, so everywhere you looked were trees. A short, stocky woman sat behind a computer, tapping on a keyboard. When I stepped up to the counter, she looked up, and then down at my wrists, her hands freezing midair.

"Demi Calloway?"

Shit. How did she know who I was?

I nodded, about to dip my head down in embarrassment, when I remembered Sage's advice and tipped my chin up.

"Yeah," I told her, voice firm. She stood, walking around her desk to greet me, and the click-clack of her heels echoed throughout the hall. When she finally stood before me, she looked me up and down and a frown tugged at her lips.

"Oh dear," she muttered, and pulled out a tablet, tapping at the screen with a stylus.

I yanked my cutoff t-shirt down to cover my belly-button, but it was no use, it sprung back up and just exposed more.

With an eye roll, the woman walked down a hallway. "Follow me, they are waiting."

They.

She said they.

Who were they?

My heart hammered against my ribcage as I passed a long hallway, all glass but tinted so I couldn't see inside.

Who cleaned this place? They must keep a hundred glass cleaners on staff. Maybe I should buy stock in Windex.

I was so lost in my thoughts about how they kept fingerprints off the windows, I didn't realize the lady had stopped, and I crashed into her back.

A growl ripped from her throat before she disguised it as a cough.

Whoa, shit.

"I'm sorry. I'm...nervous." I gave her the truth and the anger fled from her eyes. She suddenly looked at me with compassion.

"I can imagine." She gave me a weak smile and then opened the door, indicating I step inside.

I did and expected her to come with me. I mean, I didn't know this chick long, but when she closed the door and walked off back down the hall, I panicked.

Be strong.

With trepidation, I looked up at the two figures in the room.

Holy shifter.

The man standing before me was the largest male I'd ever seen. He looked like a human gorilla in size, a hulking mass of muscle so large it didn't look natural. He appeared to be in his early forties and wore a gray linen suit. Clutched in his hands was a tablet like the woman had. I did a quick and discreet whiff and recognized the wolf smell as it hit my nostrils. Gamey and earthy, it was hard to explain.

Standing beside him was...

A witch.

I'd lived with them enough to know when I was in the presence of one. It wasn't just the herbal smell they all seemed to carry, it was the lithe frame, the way they stood above you with their noses upturned as if they were better than you.

If either of them thought my clothing was atrocious, they didn't show it. Instead, the huge man just stepped forward. "Miss Calloway, I'm Eugene, head of Werewolf City Security."

Yep. I would totally give this guy the head of security job too, would hire him on the spot. He looked like he could squeeze my head between two fingers.

"Hey." I waved stupidly. His eyes flashed to my cuff and the slightest frown pulled at his lips.

"Madam Harcourt here is going to remove your cuffs and then I'll get you situated."

Remove my cuffs. He said...remove.

I so badly wanted to allow the tears that were trying to spring forth to roll down my cheeks, but I sucked those little weak droplets back.

No way was I crying in front of this giant dude and the witch. I'd wait until I was alone in my room and cry under my covers like a respectable woman, dammit.

I'd worn these cuffs since as long as I could remember. They kept a very natural part of me from being free. To remove them...it was all I'd ever wanted.

The witch strode forward. "Does the room have soundproofing? This might hurt."

I immediately backed up four paces until my back hit the wall.

Hurt. No one said anything about *hurting*.

The man just nodded, walking over to a wall panel, and suddenly a menu popped up on the glass. He tapped a few buttons and then nodded at the witch.

She looked at me, eyes narrowed. "You want them off or not? I have another appointment in fifteen minutes."

Geez, was this like a notary? She just penciled me in her little time slot? My tongue felt like sandpaper and I swallowed hard, nodding. I did want them off, so badly.

She waved me forward and I stepped slowly toward her.

"You were born outside Werewolf City?" she asked, looking down at a paper on the glass desk beside her.

I nodded.

"When were you first cuffed?" she asked.

I swallowed hard. "My first birthday was my first set. Then a second set at age five, and this set I got when I was twelve." I held them up.

They never hurt to take off before, when the witches changed me out for a bigger set, so I was wondering why they would now.

"They never hurt to remove before..."

She raised an eyebrow. "That's because they weren't removing the *magic* in them, just changing out the metal to grow with your form. I'll be stripping the spell that's been attached to your body for the last..." She paused, looking at the sheet of paper, "Twenty years. This will most *definitely* hurt."

Fuck. My wolf rose to the surface then, and I knew my eyes had gone yellow. Silverish white pelts of fur rippled down my arms and the witch stepped back a pace, looking at the gorilla man, Eugene.

"She...shouldn't be able to do that..." she said with a frown.

The pelts of fur hit the cuffs at my wrists and electricity shot up my arms, causing me to cry out.

They both looked uncomfortably at each other, unsure what to do.

Eugene tapped something on his tablet. "She's been reported to the principal's office..." He paused and then looked at me. Was that pride in his gaze? "Three hundred and ninety times for showing signs of near shifting."

I tried to keep the grin off my face. My parents never near shifted. Other than some occasional yellow eyes, their wolves were kept pretty much in control by the cuffs, unlike mine.

The witch scoffed. "Well, whomever did her original spell was an idiot. Who was it?"

He looked at his tablet again. "Belladonna Mongrave. Your high priestess."

Her cheeks pinked and she waved him off. "No matter. It's coming off anyway."

A black satchel sat on the edge of the table and she reached inside, pulling out a copper knife.

I flinched, my wolf rising to the surface again with my fear, but I shoved her down.

If I did this, went through with the pain, I could be free. I could finally, for the first time in my life... shift.

Eugene placed his tablet on the table and came up behind me. "I'm just going to hold you in place so that you don't move and get a main artery cut," he told me.

What?

"Main artery cut" were three words I *never* wanted to hear again.

I nodded, tears filling my eyes as the fear became too much.

When his strong hands gripped my forearms and offered the cuffs up to the witch with my wrists facing the ceiling, it took every ounce of control I had to not bite him and fight him off.

I felt the anxiety and panic fill my body as this situation brought me into a dark memory, a memory I didn't even think about anymore, something so horrific I'd locked it away, only glimpsing it when I was put into situations where I felt cornered, trapped.

Eugene's hands pinning down my arms took me back to that awful night six years ago. My breath became shaky as I fought the flashback assaulting my mind. The black silk bedsheets, the four vampire males, the blood…

I shook my head, trying to clear the thoughts as a whimper ripped from my throat.

I'm okay, I'm okay, I'm okay, I chanted inside my head, knowing that Eugene didn't intend to hurt me, that he was actually trying to help me.

I was finally going to be free. To be a wolf, to shift whenever I wanted…I couldn't even comprehend such a thing.

My mother and father were cuffed too, so before today, I'd never actually seen a werewolf in wolf form until seeing the students lying on the grass. I could do this.

Just thinking of my parents sent sadness sinking into my stomach like a stone. What time was it? Were they home from work? Wondering where I was? Was Raven telling them right now? I tried to focus on them and ignore the panic attack that had me in its grip. Whatever pain was about to befall me was going to be worth it to be free.

The witch brought the copper dagger to the cuff and sliced downward, causing it to open and fall to the floor. I flinched, bracing myself for the pain, but nothing happened. She did the same to the other cuff, and it cut like it was made of butter...but caused me no pain. A sigh of relief went through me. Then she placed her hand over my chest, palm splayed out until her nails were digging into my skin.

Hard.

"Entora dilumin wolven forchesto," she began to chant.

Witch speak.

I knew enough of it to pick up the words *wolf death*.

Before I could dwell too much on the wording, searing pain ripped through my chest. I bucked in Eugene's arms but he pinned my back to his chest and it was like I was being held in cement.

Panic and pain swirled within me, and I had to bite my tongue to keep from screaming.

The witch took the copper blade and held it to my hair. Using one hand, she cut a chunk off and then placed the hair under her palm, which was still on my chest. I was in too much pain to care that she'd just given me a hack-job haircut. What was once a sharp jabbing pain in my chest now reached down my spine and into my toes.

"Stop!" I wailed, fearing I was about to pass out. Sweat prickled on my skin and my wolf rose to the surface, my teeth lengthening in my mouth.

Whoa.

"Wolven risenoto becara," she whispered, and that's when I died.

I mean, it felt like I'd died. It felt like a fucking semi-truck ran me over on the road and then I'd been put into a blender. I must have fainted, because when I came to, I was slack in Eugene's arms. He was holding me up by the armpits and the witch was across the room washing her hands with hand sanitizer like touching me was gross.

"You okay?" Eugene huffed in my ear, his voice laced with compassion.

I nodded against his chest and he deposited me into a chair. My whole body dropped into the seat like a sack of flour and I just sat there panting, trying to catch my breath. My skin felt like I'd been left out in the sun too long, and I had a feeling I was going to be sore tomorrow.

"Payment," the witch muttered, holding out her phone to the giant man.

Eugene tapped something on his tablet, casting worried glances my way, and her phone beeped. She looked down at it and smiled. "Pleasure doing business with you."

He glared at her as she left the room, the door softly closing behind her.

I stared at the cuffs, sliced in half and lying on the floor. Then I looked at my wrists. They were white, like butt white where the cuffs had been, and golden tan everywhere else. At the edges were scars from the constant rubbing over the years, the constant shocks.

I was free...

Eugene seemed to notice my distress and cleared his throat, picking the cuffs up off the floor and walking over to the trash can.

"No! I want to keep them," I blurted. I didn't know why but throwing them in the trash felt like throwing a part of me away.

He nodded, setting them on the glass desk in front of me.

There was a light tap on the door and he seemed to be expecting it. Standing, he tapped something on the glass menu board and spoke. "Come in."

The front desk lady was back with her tablet. She took one look at the cutoff cuffs on the table and raised an eyebrow. Then she took a seat across from me and tapped on her tablet with record speed. "Okay Miss Calloway—"

"Call me Demi, please. My mom is Mrs. Calloway."

She nodded. "You have been entered into the system here. I'm just arranging your school schedule. What do you want to be your major?"

My *major*? That was absolutely the last thing on my mind. At Delphi, I was a business major because that's all they would allow me. Everything else was too witchy or too far suited for one of the other magical races. Wolves never got banished, so they didn't have wolf curriculum I guess. Whatever that would be.

"What...do you have?" I hedged.

She handed me the tablet and I started to scroll.

Lycan surgeon.

Physical therapy.

Cosmetology.

When my eyes landed on photography, I nearly squealed. I had a pretty loyal following on Instagram because of my photos. I *loved* taking pictures. When I was behind the camera, something inside of me came alive. I could see the world in a different way.

"Photography please." I handed it back.

She frowned and shared a look with Eugene before looking back at me. "If you are to be a potential suitor to Sawyer Hudson, then you can only minor in photography and would need a more respectable major."

I snort-laughed, but quickly covered it when I realized she was serious.

Okay…gotta keep up with the lie that this was the reason I was here. Sawyer was a cool dude who took pity on me. I wouldn't want him to get into trouble.

"Do you have a business major?"

Relief crossed her face. "Yes. Good choice."

She tapped away at her tablet and then looked to Eugene. "Do you think we have enough guards at Emory Hall if I place her there?"

She was talking about the dorms. Why would *I* need guards?

"Actually…I was hoping to be at Lexington. Near suite eleven?" I threw as much charm into my voice as possible, remembering what Sage had said about taking me under her wing.

The woman looked at Eugene, and he nodded once.

Then she tapped her tablet a few more times. "I have the suite across the hall recently available. Number ten."

I didn't want to know why it was "recently" available, I was just glad I might actually have one friend here.

After a few more minutes, she held up her phone in my face. "Smile."

What?

Oh geez, a picture? Right now? I was still sweaty from my panic attack and dying.

I gave her a lame smile and she tapped the screen before setting the phone down. Peering over her shoulder, I looked at the pic she'd snapped.

Oh man, that was pretty bad. Hopefully just for her records or something.

A few moments later there was a knock at the door and a tall but scrawny older man entered holding a black leather backpack. He placed it in front of me and then handed me a credit card type of key card. "Don't ever lose this. It's your key into everything," he told me and left.

I glanced at the key card.

Fuck my life.

A two-inch square showed my scared and fake smiling face, with Hot Mess haircut.

Awesome.

"In the bag will be a tablet with your class schedule, map of the campus, school, Werewolf City bylaws, and anything else you should need." She tapped the black leather backpack. "There is a food app where you can order meal service to your room, and there are electric scooters and bikes all over campus. Just swipe your key card and take whatever one you want."

Okay…I'd officially reached information overload. This was too much, and clearly *expensive.*

"And…how much will all of this cost me?" I gestured around the room.

She looked offended, sharing a scandalous glance at Eugene. "All expenses associated with the females that are invited to school here during the mating year are paid for by the alpha."

Holy shit, I was *totally* on *Werewolf Bachelor.*

Just breathe.

"Even if he doesn't pick me?" I hedged, "Like, do I have to pay it all back?" Because obviously he wasn't going to pick me. I was fucking twenty-one years old. I wasn't ready for marriage. I didn't even want to be picked. Mostly. I mean he was hot, I'd give him that. Being picked wouldn't be the *worst* thing to ever happen to me. But this whole thing was nuts.

"One second." She tapped her screen. "There, I've signed you up for etiquette classes. A lady *never* talks about money." She patted my hand and stood.

Ouch, did I just get burned by some old lady wearing pumps and pantyhose?

When she left the room, I stared at Eugene incredulously.

He only smirked. "She's one of the elites. Born of money, likes having an important job. She doesn't understand people like us."

People like us.

When I didn't say anything, he leaned forward. "My dad was the Werewolf Elementary School janitor and my mom the lunch lady. The only reason I got this job is because I'm built like a truck and I win every fight I get in."

I grinned. I liked him immediately. I liked everyone here so far. My parents made it sound like some dark and scary place they'd had to flee.

"Sawyer pays for everything," he told me. "It's never a question and you won't pay a dime back, no matter what happens. It's all in the bylaws." He tapped the backpack.

I guess I had some reading to do.

He stood and gestured to the door. "You can go. You missed the first day, but classes start eight a.m. sharp, and Sawyer will be picking his first date tomorrow night at the dinner gala."

My eyes widened.

Picking a date?

Dinner gala?

Freaking Werewolf Bachelor.

"Umm, gala usually means a dress...right?" I gestured to my clothes.

He pointed to the backpack. "Check the campus map. There's a mall behind the tennis courts that has everything ladies like to wear. Use your key card to pay. Sawyer picks up the bill, no questions asked."

What. The. *Fuck*. Was. Happening?

At this point I just felt stupid for asking questions, so I nodded and stood. "Thanks for um..." I pointed to the broken cuffs and shoved them in the bag. "Everything."

He tipped his head, standing as well. "In twenty years of serving the alpha, I've never seen him get in a fight with his son. Until today. Sawyer fought for you. Don't *ever* forget that."

Then he walked out and left me shocked.

Sawyer fought for me? Those words stuck with me all the way to Lexington Hall.

CHAPTER THREE

LEXINGTON HALL WAS CLEAR ACROSS CAMPUS AND I rode a badass electric scooter to get there. This place was amazing. Minus all of the assholes who kept staring at me and whispering. It took me four tries to get the dorm door open, until some blond waved her key at a little square thingy and it opened automatically. I stepped in behind her into a large entryway with a concierge type of woman sitting behind a desk. She had a phone to her ear. When she saw me, she hung up and flagged me down with a flustered look on her face.

"Miss Calloway?"

I nodded. "They didn't put your food preferences in. My chef needs to know, are you vegetarian? Gluten free? What are your dietary restrictions?"

I forced myself not to laugh. "None, ma'am."

She frowned. "Paleo? Keto?"

Keta what?

"Umm. I like all food."

This seemed to confuse her and her eyebrows drew into a frown. "No special diet, then?"

I shrugged. "Pizza, pasta, chicken sandwiches."

Her eyes ran over my body and she seemed...I don't know what she seemed, but I was confused. Luckily, Sage popped into view and saved me from further embarrassment.

"She's normal, Kendra. *Normal* food," Sage told her, speaking the last two words slowly like Kendra didn't understand.

The front desk woman glared at Sage and waved her off. "Very well."

Sage looped her arm through mine and leaned in closely. "All of the 'prospective girls' are on special diets to be rail thin for my cousin."

"Gross," I said. My thighs definitely jiggled when I walked and my nickname all through middle school, before Wolf Girl, was Bubble Butt.

"Eugene texted me that you would be across the hall from me. Have you eaten dinner?"

I shook my head, taking in all the girls walking around in high heels and the luxury of the open entry room.

"We can go to the mall and go shopping so you have clothes to wear to school tomorrow. We can grab a bite to eat there. Or you can just borrow mine and we can order in."

Eugene texted her? He probably guarded her too since she was... I dunno, were they royal? She was the alpha's niece, so obviously that was special. My head was spinning. I *did* need clothes, like...I didn't even have extra underwear. They basically kidnapped me midday without any of my stuff.

"Sure...um, let me just freshen up. Call my parents."

She nodded. "Meet you in the lobby in thirty minutes?"

I gave her a thumbs-up and then she gestured down the hall. "You're on the first floor, down to the right."

I started to walk that way, and she broke off to talk to some girls who were playing ping pong. I was pleased to see that the bedroom doors were not in fact made of glass. A few of them were open and girls were sitting on each other's beds talking, but they quieted when I passed. Suite eight, suite nine, suite—

There was a tall blond leaning against my doorframe, wearing a feral grin. My wolf immediately rose to the surface as the blond pushed off the door and looked me up and down. "This is the girl Sawyer begged his dad to free from banishment? Hmm, I expected more." She stalked a slow circle around me, looking at me like I was a piece of trash.

A low growl rose in my throat, and she matched it with a growl of her own. Stepping forward quickly, she forced me to back up until my back slammed against the door.

"Sawyer and I dated for two years. He only broke up with me because the bylaws state you must be single when you enter your mating year. He's *mine*, so don't even think about entertaining this as anything other than a charity case."

She'd caged me against the door and my wolf did *not* like it.

"Back. Up." Fur rippled down my arms, but she didn't look scared or surprised, she looked...excited.

"Meredith! I thought that was your *shrill* voice I heard," Sage called out as she barreled down the hallway.

Meredith, aka Darth Vader, backed up then and plastered a fake smile on her face. "Sage. Hey, girl!" Her voice held so much fakeness it made me sick. "Just welcoming our new little *friend*."

"How *sweet* of you." Obvious sarcasm dripped from Sage's voice. "Brittney is asking for you."

Meredith gave me one last venomous look and then turned and left with Sage following after her.

Bitch fight averted.

Using my key card, I slipped into the room, shutting the door behind me as the auto lock clicked into place.

When I looked up at the room, the breath caught in my throat.

I was in a Las Vegas penthouse. At least that's what this looked like. Travertine floors, fine linens, rich woods, and a huge standing mirror.

"Holy shit," I whispered as I stepped into the master

with an attached bathroom. A huge soaking tub with a rain shower and vanity counter sat along the wall. There was a giant walk-in closet that I would never have enough clothes for. I walked back into the living room and checked out the flat screen TV on the wall in front of a small two-seater couch. This wasn't a dorm, it was a luxury apartment.

On the coffee table in front of the couch was a small gift basket and note. I picked up the note and scanned it. There was a typed paragraph that was a generic welcome from Sawyer to the mating selection year, but someone had crossed it out with a big X. Along the bottom was written:

I couldn't let you stay in that place.

Sawyer.

Emotion tightened my throat.

I couldn't let you stay in that place.

I knew literally nothing about Sawyer, except that he was kind, and I would never forget that. He'd seen a fellow wolf in a bad situation and took pity on me, and I would have to find a nice way to thank him.

In the gift basket was a collection of teas, cookies, and dried fruits. It was sweet, but I couldn't really focus on it. I needed to call my parents. They were no doubt losing their damn minds.

Holding my phone in my hand, I powered it up.

Sixty-eight missed calls and thirty texts. All the calls were my parents and all the texts were Raven. With a shaky hand, I dialed my mom's cell.

She picked up on the first ring. "Demi Calloway! Tell me this is a prank."

I gulped. "No, Mom. I'm at Sterling Hill—"

"Demi!" my dad yelled—I was clearly on speakerphone. "You left without telling us?"

I was quiet for a moment. I never thought they would be mad...all they ever talked about was how much easier life would be if we were back in Werewolf City. Now I had my chance.

"I had sixty seconds to decide. I thought you would want this for me."

Two heavy sighs reached through the phone and into my heart.

"We do," my mom said. "We do, hun."

"We just never expected it," my father cut in. "We assumed our banishment extended to you forever."

I blew air out through my lips. "Maybe it did... I dunno, but then I met the alpha's son, Sawyer, at Delphi, and...a few hours later I was being invited here. Now I have a room, and everything is paid for and it's *wild*."

Silence.

"Mom?"

"I know...I was a mating year girl too. It's nice, they give you a nice life." Her voice sounded hollow.

Why did she sound sad? OMG, did she almost marry Sawyer's dad?

"What happened?" I asked her. "Did you and the alpha...?"

"No. I never even made the top twenty." She laughed nervously but it didn't sound real.

"Mom?"

"Yes, hun?"

"Why did you and Dad get banished? You made this place sound awful, but it doesn't seem so bad."

I was afraid I was going to hear about it from someone like Meredith, and I wanted to hear it from them instead. I'd asked a handful of times over the past decade and always got the same answer.

Silence.

"Tell her." My father's voice was low.

"No, dammit," she growled at my father, and chills ran the length of my arms. It must be worse than I thought; they never argued.

"Mom. I'm twenty-one, I'm not a kid anymore." Whatever it was, I deserved to hear it from my own parents.

She sighed. "I can't. I'm not ready."

Holy shit...this whole time I'd been told we were banished because of something my father did, but now I wondered if it was in fact my mother.

My hands shook. "Mom, you're scaring me."

"I'll tell you when I'm ready," she said. "Your

father and I are surprised but happy for you. Even if Sawyer doesn't pick you, you'll get a top-notch education, a great job upon graduation, and a nice house in Werewolf City. It's great news...we're just shocked is all."

I knew she was trying to steer things away from talking about her, so I let her. "How many window washers does this place have?" I went for humor and was rewarded with her laughter, followed by my father's. I'd give her a week or so to settle into the idea that I was here and then I needed to know everything. We made a bit more small talk before we hung up and I promised to call them every day.

When I left the room, I found Sage leaning against the hallway wall tapping on her phone. "Ready to shop until you drop?"

I laughed nervously. "Not really." The most shopping I ever did was like fifty dollars at the thrift store. It could take hours to get decent thrift store finds, but when you stumbled across a vintage Beatles shirt autographed in silver sharpie...you struck gold. You also never machine washed that shirt in case it washed off the autograph, so instead you drowned it in perfume and hand rinsed it gently, avoiding the pen markings.

She waved me off. "Don't let your little run-in with Meredith get you down. She's like that to everyone."

I'd forgotten my run-in with Meredith until that moment. I was actually more worried about spending someone else's money. "I'm not used to shopping," I confessed.

She nodded. "I'll help you. It will be fun!"

Three hours, thirty-six pieces of sushi, and five shopping bags full later, we exited the mall.

"I can't believe I just spent two grand of someone else's money." My eyes were wide as we loaded my bags onto the back of an electric scooter.

Sage waved me off. "I do it all the time on my dad's card. It's fine. The cards have a daily limit and it didn't get declined, so that means we did good."

I snorted. We had very, very different upbringings. I gestured to the bags. "I only got one fancy dress. Think that's enough?" The rest were ripped jeans, shorts, tank-tops, and sneakers, and a few flowy bohemian dresses. I also got makeup, a flat iron, and some cool purses with studs on them.

Sage gave me a conspiratorial look. "You want to stand out? Don't dress like the lemmings here. Seriously, my cousin picked you for a reason. I think he digs the t-shirt and jean shorts vibe."

She motioned to my outfit.

I chuckled, but the smile fell from my lips. Sage was becoming a good friend and I didn't want to lie to her. "You know your cousin doesn't *really* like me. He just pulled all that because it was the only way to get me out of banishment and he feels bad for me."

Sage looked at me like I was five years old. "Aww, is that what he told you? Cute." She booped my nose and a warm feeling settled into my stomach. What did that mean? Did it mean that...Sawyer wanted me here, like to *date* me?

Was I really in the *Werewolf Bachelor* running? Did I even want to be? I thought of his intense blue eyes and the way he'd seen me lose my shit. It was a weak moment for me, a moment of struggle that highlighted how badly I'd been treated while being forced to live out life in banishment. He saw all of that and...he still liked me?

Oh man. Shit just got real.

We rode back to the dorm and Sage helped me to my door with all my bags. She yawned, squeezing my shoulder. "I had fun today. You're cool."

I gave her a smile. "Me too. Thanks for taking me shopping."

She nodded and waved me good night before slipping into her room across the hall.

I was about to go into my own room when my wolf rose to the surface and I paused in the door frame.

It hit me then...in that moment.

I was *free*.

I could go outside, shift into my wolf, and run for the first time *ever*. And that's exactly what my wolf wanted me to do. With a grin, I shut my door, grabbed my key card, and all but ran to the exit of the dorm.

The front desk lady, Kendra, looked at me but said nothing. I was an adult after all and this was basically college, college *Werewolf Bachelor* style. Slipping outside, I breathed in the cool night air.

A run with my wolf, I couldn't conceive of it before. I was giddy with excitement.

I burst across the lawn, smiling as the cold night wind ripped through my hair. There were a few students heading back into the dorms. The moon was high in the sky, casting a soft light upon the thick forest that encompassed the school grounds. I slipped into the first thicket of trees I saw and started to disrobe, preparing to shift. I knew enough about being a werewolf that it would tear my clothes if I didn't shift naked. Reaching down, I grabbed the hem of my shirt, and pulled it up over my head just as a man cleared his throat.

With a yelp, I pulled the shirt back down, covering my stomach.

"Sorry...I, uh...saw you undressing and figured I should let you know I was here." I knew that voice, even after only meeting him once.

I spun and saw Sawyer, shirtless and in low-slung sweatpants.

Holy mother of abs...

My eyes raked over his chiseled chest and my ability to form words flew from my brain.

"Going for a run?" he asked, pointing to the forest.

I just nodded dumbly, trying not to drool, and then held up my cuff-less wrists. "First time."

A frown pulled at his lips and he nodded in understanding. "I was going to go too. Want to join me or would you rather be alone?"

Truth be told, I was terrified. I'd never shifted before. It would be nice to have someone to do that with...but *him*?

I swallowed hard. "I don't...really know what I'm doing. Like...I don't even know how to shift; I wouldn't want to slow you down."

I knew that racing in wolf form was a big bragging right if you were the fastest. My mom talked about the good old days all the time, when she used to run my dad ragged around the campus when they went here.

Shame colored my cheeks, but he didn't give me a pitying look. He nodded once, curtly. Moving across the space to stand closer to me, I watched as his muscles danced under his skin.

Lord have *mercy*. He was quite literally the hottest guy I'd ever seen. And I was pretty sure he knew it.

"You could never slow me down," he whispered as my throat went dry. Then he moved to stand at my back and I felt the heat from his body press against mine. "Undress and I'll walk you through it. I'll stay turned away until your shift is complete."

Everything inside of me clenched when he said

"undress." I know he didn't mean it like that, but... damn.

I cleared my throat, looking behind me to make sure his back was in fact to me.

It was.

"Okay." My voice cracked and I hated myself for it. I was *not* a boy-crazy girl. Never had been. You either wanted to be with me, and that was cool, or not. I always knew where I stood and I didn't chase men. This *Werewolf Bachelor* was like my worst fucking nightmare. Did he like me? Did he like fifty other women? Was I just here because of some bylaw or because he wanted to date me?

Without over thinking it too much, I pulled my shirt off and tossed it on a nearby flat rock. Blowing air through my teeth, I unclipped my bra and tossed that next. My inner wolf's desire to run was overshadowing my fear at being naked in front of Sawyer, even if he wasn't looking. I was sure they all grew up being naked all the time and it was no big deal, but it was to me. He seemed to understand that. It seemed like he was a great guy, which was rare in my experience.

"Sawyer?" I tossed my panties on the nearby rock and stood completely naked.

"Yeah?" His voice had dropped three octaves and I wasn't sure if it was because he'd seen me throw the panties or not, but the desire in his voice was *thick*. It brought heat right to my core.

I just realized that I'd never thanked him for his rescue from Delphi, from the cuffs. "Thanks for...getting me out of that place."

Silence.

When he finally spoke, his voice was husky and serious: "You belong with us."

Us. He meant the werewolf species of course, but damn at this point I was totally hoping for a rose at tomorrow night's dinner. I wanted more of him, to get to know him better before he married some perfect preppy woman and I never saw him again.

"What if...I can't shift?" I croaked.

I mean twenty years in magical handcuffs surely broke my wolf, no?

As if answering that thought, my wolf stirred to the surface and Sawyer laughed, a bright trilling sound that had butterflies turning in my stomach.

"The girl I saw today...her wolf is alive and well and waiting to be freed."

His confidence in me was sexy as hell, but now I felt performance anxiety. What if I half shifted and got stuck? It had happened before, my parents told me about it. Or what if I just sort of grew fur but nothing else and was a furry human?

Only one way to find out, I guess.

"Okay. I'm ready," I told him before I lost my nerve.

"All right, close your eyes." His voice was smooth

and deep and so damn distractingly sexy. Talking to someone without looking at them was a total turn on.

With a shaky breath, I did as he said. Standing here, naked, eyes closed, back-to-back with the alpha's son in the middle of the woods was hands down the weirdest thing I'd ever done.

"Imagine you are driving a car, your hands are at the wheel. Look down at your hands."

What the what? Okay...was this some New Age visualization shit?

I did as he asked.

"For over twenty years *you* have been the one driving the car, *you've* been in control," he said, and I wasn't sure if it was my imagination or if he moved the slightest bit closer to me, because I felt more warmth at my back. "It's time to let *her* drive. Let your wolf take the wheel, watch as your hands turn to claws."

I swallowed hard, pulling my thoughts away from his sexy voice and back to the hands on the wheel.

I'm ready to let you drive, I said to my inner self, my wolf. Then I visualized my human hands on a steering wheel and watched as my fingers lengthened to claws. Fur puffed out on the top of my hands and my bones cracked.

"Now let go. Just let it all go. *Lose control*," he whispered.

My whole life had been an exercise in control. Don't shift, don't show your fur, don't let your teeth lengthen, don't this, don't that, and for the first time ever I just dropped it all. Like a brick wall being smashed to bits, I let it all come tumbling down.

A scream ripped from my throat as pain flared along my spine and I flew forward onto all fours. Fire ripped through me, pain mixed with heat.

"Breathe through the change. Your wolf knows what to do," he said from behind me.

"Everything...*hurts*," I panted, my voice barely human.

A cool hand landed on my back and my entire body melted under his pressure. Everything within me relaxed then, and that's when it happened. I'd never forget the sound of my own bones snapping. It was a sharp sound that came from within me and outside of me at the same time. The heat lessened, as well as the pain, and I just... transformed. The fur I was used to popping up on my arms flared to life on my entire body. I literally felt my face grow as my nose protruded into my line of sight and I saw that it was a white silvery fur. My tongue rolled out of my mouth as I panted to cool myself off. When I looked down, I saw four white and gray paws.

"Oh fuck..." Sawyer's voice behind me was like sandpaper.

Okay...not the reaction I expected. More like, "Your wolf is beautiful," or, "I really like your markings." I spun around, to see what was wrong and a terrified howl ripped from my throat.

What. The. Hell?

Sawyer stood over my naked body, my naked human body. I was curled into a ball at his feet.

My heart pounded frantically in my wolf chest as I shook my head. I was a wolf looking at my human form, then I was my human looking at my wolf.

What the hell was happening? Was I dreaming, was I hallucinating?

My human form sat up, draped both arms across her chest, and looked at me with two wide blue eyes.

"Not...possible." Sawyer knelt beside my human form, looking at her with a slack jaw. I was shaking from shock and he wrapped a warm arm around me, tucking me into his chest.

I blinked and then I was looking at everything from my human perspective, nuzzled into him, shaking as my teeth chattered.

What was happening?

I was...two people.

Split?

"Sawyer!" a male voice yelled from the trees, and he stiffened.

His voice was frantic: "You have to shift back."

I just curled into him, naked, fragile, scared.

He put his hand out to my wolf as if he were calling a dog. Then my wolf walked forward and I looked down to see my furry paws. I was back in her perspective and it was as easy as blinking.

"Sawyer!" The male voice was closer now, and it was followed by another voice and another. It must be his guards looking for him. He was basically royalty.

My wolf leaned forward and smelled his hand.

The second I got close, his hand snaked out and grabbed my wolf by the scruff, pulling me up to meet his gaze, his eyes sharpened.

"Shift. Back. Now. Or they'll kill you both," he growled, alpha power pressing down on my body at his command.

Pain sliced along my tailbone and the heat was back. It felt like I'd just been sucked into a vacuum; there was pressure all around me as a force slammed into my back, like I'd been hit with a baseball bat, then my eyelids snapped open, and Sawyer was looking at me with relief. Bringing my hands up to my face, I saw that they were human.

"Sawyer!" a man yelled as Sawyer pulled me up and tucked me behind his back to shield me from view.

Just then, Brandon from the van ride earlier, along with Walsh, stepped into the clearing, holding guns at their sides. The giant lead guard, Eugene, stepped up right behind them.

They took one look at me, naked and hiding behind Sawyer, who had his shirt off, and then gave us their backs, cheeks flaming red.

One of the guards mumbled, "We heard a wolf howl, it sounded like it was in distress...we thought you were..."

"I'm fine. We went for a run." His voice cracked. "Give us a moment," he commanded and they immediately began to walk away.

"Get dressed," he called to me, keeping his back to me, as if he didn't just see me freaking naked. Oh my God, I wanted to die right now. My hands shook as I slipped into my panties and bra, then put my shirt over my head and zipped my shorts up.

I didn't know a ton about werewolves, but I knew enough to know what just happened wasn't fucking normal. Like...at all.

When I was finally dressed, I just cleared my throat and he turned around. I couldn't meet his eyes, I was so...embarrassed, horrified, scared.

Reaching out, he grasped my chin in his warm fingers and tipped it up to meet his piercing blue eyes.

"Don't tell *anyone* what just happened. Your life depends on it, you understand?"

My life?

Oh God.

Tears filled my eyes and I nodded.

"No one," he pressed. "Not your parents, not Sage, no one. And don't shift again, not without me there."

I swallowed hard. "What...was that?"

He sighed, releasing my chin, and ran his hands through his hair. "Give me time to look into this." But I could see it in his face...he knew. He knew something and wasn't telling me.

"Sawyer. What am I?" My voice was firmer this time and I could see the pity in his eyes.

He tucked a lock of blond hair behind my ear, looking sad, like he'd just received bad news. "You're amazing."

That wasn't what I wanted to hear. I wanted to hear him tell me how the hell my wolf and I just split in two. I never should have come back here. Was it too late to rewind the last few hours and go back to my old life? Because clearly this was a mistake.

CHAPTER FOUR

I TOSSED AND TURNED ALL NIGHT, BARELY SLEEPING. I kept dreaming of my wolf and human, lying five feet apart from each other. Then I remembered Sawyer saying my life depended on no one finding out what I was, and I woke up panting, covered in sweat. This happened over a dozen times throughout the night until finally I awoke to my alarm blaring near my head.

My first waking thought was Sawyer saying, "*You're amazing.*"

I sighed, hugging my knees as I buried my head between my legs.

He saw me naked. For some reason that was the sticking point from last night. Screw the fact that I was some kind of freak split shifter.

Sawyer. Hudson. Saw. Me. Naked.

"Rise and shine, bitch!" I recognized Sage's voice

from behind my door. I groaned, shuffling over to the door and wrenching it open. She held two cups of to-go coffee, and after looking me up and down, winced. "Bad night? You look like shit, and the first meet and greet gala is tonight."

Screw the gala! I wanted to scream at her. *I'm a split shifting freak and Sawyer saw me naked!*

She handed me the coffee and I chugged it. Warm, sweet liquid rushed down my throat and I pulled my shit together. Everything was going to be fine. I just wouldn't shift anymore, I didn't shift for over twenty years and I survived life okay...

Only now I was living with a wolf pack and I wasn't known for keeping my temper in check.

But whatever, everything would be *fine*.

A grin pulled across her face when I didn't say anything. "So you're *not* gonna tell me your little secret?"

My heart leapt into my throat and I swallowed hard. "What?"

She waved me off, pushing her way inside. "Brandon texted me this morning that he caught you and my cousin naked in the woods last night! You little slut."

Relief washed through me as heat flared in my cheeks. "He was helping me shift for the first time. I ran into him randomly."

And he was super sweet and understanding about the whole thing.

She winked. "I love it."

I rolled my eyes. "I'm going to jump in the shower. I'll be ready in five, you can wait on the couch if you want." I gestured for her to sit, actually excited that she thought we were good enough friends to come over in the morning before my first class.

She nodded. "I'll pick out your outfit. You might see Sawyer at breakfast."

My eyes widened.

Sawyer.

Last night.

There was no way he would pick me for anything now. He was probably regretting bringing me here in the first place. I absolutely prayed I never saw him again.

After a quick shower in which I somehow shaved, brushed my teeth, and washed my hair in four minutes, I came out to see a clothing bomb had exploded on my bed.

Sage had curated a pretty badass outfit that was totally my style. Light-wash ripped jean shorts, black vintage soft tee, and studded leather backpack purse. There was even a black leather studded headband to match.

"You need to wear the heels or this is just too grungy." Sage pointed to a pair of black studded stiletto boots that weren't mine.

I shook my head. "Then I guess I'm grungy," I said as I slipped into my white Converse knockoffs that I scored at the goodwill. They were so comfortable and I just couldn't deal with breaking my neck today on top of all the other drama.

Sage rolled her eyes. "Fine, but obviously heels for the gala?"

I shrugged. "Definitely a dress."

Sage grinned, and in that moment I could see her resemblance to Sawyer. "I hope my cousin picks you. My aunt and uncle will have a heart attack."

"Gee, thanks." I grabbed my brush and ran it through my long damp hair. "Trust me. This is a charity case, and after last night he won't be picking me."

Sage took the brush from me and started to detangle the back while I threw on lip gloss and mascara.

"Keep telling yourself that. If anything, last night sealed the deal."

Her words stayed with me all the way to the dining hall. Last night had been intense, the way Sawyer grabbed the scruff of my wolf's neck and commanded her to shift. I'd felt the alpha power wash over me, something he and his father both had. I trusted him. I could tell he was trying to protect me. He'd said he was going to look into this, but something told me he already knew what it all meant, he knew how I could shift like that but he wouldn't tell me, which meant it was really bad.

We waited in the food line and I grabbed an omelet

and some toast. All of the food was really fancy, buffet style, and at the end of the line I just swiped my little key card and it was paid for.

So weird.

When we were done, Sage scanned the tables and that's when I saw him.

Sawyer.

Sitting with Meredith.

Eugene was standing a few feet from the table, and a line of five or six girls had lined up behind him, writing their name on a clipboard.

Oh my God. Were they…lining up to eat with him?

"That's disgusting," I observed as Sage started to weave through the tables.

She followed my gaze. "Oh, get used to it. Sawyer needs to pick a wife by the end of the year or he can't inherit the alpha position."

My eyes widened. "Really? They force him to get married?"

Sage shrugged. "They strongly encourage him to pick a mate who will bear strong children." She winked.

Gross. What a weird society, but clearly, from the looks of the other girls waiting to have five minutes with him, it was totally normal. I wondered if I'd grown up here, if I would think it was normal too.

I realized too late that she was heading for their table.

"No, I don't want to—"

Sawyer looked up from his conversation with

Meredith and saw me walking behind Sage. His eyes roamed up and down my body and my cheeks warmed. Sage plopped her tray right next to Meredith and took a seat.

"Hey, cuz." She pulled a piece of fruit from his plate and popped it in her mouth. He reached over and used his hand to rough up her hair, which caused her to growl and swat at him.

Meredith looked at Sage with annoyance. "Still acting like you guys are twelve, I see." I stood there like an idiot, clutching my tray and looking for an open seat at another table when he spoke.

"Demi, sit next to me." Sawyer patted the open bench beside him and Meredith froze. Her back was to me, and I didn't think she realized I was there.

Not wanting to make a scene, I strode forward, passed the line of girls who now wanted to murder me, and set my tray next to Sawyer.

"Sleep okay?" He looked over at me as he chewed on a piece of bacon. His dark hair was slicked into a perfect quaff and he looked freshly shaven.

No. Not at all. You saw me naked and I'm a freak. "Yeah." My voice cracked as I nervously picked up a piece of toast.

"Carbs?" Meredith asked as she watched me take a bite of the bread. "Someone doesn't want to fit into their gala dress," she said with a snicker.

Fur rippled down my arms, then Sawyer's hand

snaked out under the table and clenched my bare thigh, immediately subduing my wolf.

Holy shit, I almost shifted.

I was so used to having those cuffs on and having to push my wolf out so hard that I nearly shifted from a stupid comment. I needed to get myself under control.

Meredith looked at my once hairy arms and rolled her eyes. "She's like a wolf pup who can't control herself."

"So," Sage interrupted, looking right at Sawyer. "I heard you two were found naked in the woods together last night?" Sage looked from Sawyer to me, grinning, and caused Meredith's mouth to pop open in shock.

"Sage," Sawyer growled, but was that a grin on his lips?

Meredith stood. "I think my five minutes is up. See you tonight, Sawyer." Then she waltzed off, leaving her tray, and swished her hips across the room.

He released his hand from my thigh and I found that I was sad to see it go, before rubbing his temples. "What did I ever see in that woman?"

"Nice boobs? Looks good in a bikini?" Sage offered, and Sawyer pinned her with a glare.

"Thousands of dollars in etiquette classes and you say the most shocking things," he commented.

I relaxed a little now that Darth Vader was gone.

"So, Demi, what major are you taking?" Sawyer turned to me and I realized that he'd seen me naked but knew nothing about me. My eyes scanned over his perfect face. Dark hair and searing blue eyes were my kryptonite.

"Well, I wanted photography, but apparently that doesn't make good wife material? So I am only minoring in it and majoring in business." I dug into my second piece of buttered toast.

Sage grinned. "This is why I like her. She tells it like it is."

Sawyer frowned, his brows drawing together. "They told you what to major in?"

I nodded. "I also got signed up for etiquette classes for asking how much the school tuition would cost me."

Sage snort-laughed and Sawyer's frown deepened. "Shit. I'm sorry. I should have told you more before bringing you here." There was genuine regret in his voice, which I thought was sweet.

I shrugged. "Better than where I was."

Silence descended on the table as he no doubt thought about seeing me at Delphi. I remembered the desperate scream as I'd howled, not able to shift into my wolf. But now that I was free, I couldn't shift for other reasons.

Sawyer looked sideways at me. "Photography, huh? Can I see any of your work? Do you have a portfolio?"

Nerves gnawed at my gut. "I mean, nothing professional, but I'm on Insta."

"Sawyer doesn't do social media," Sage interrupted before she shoved more food into her mouth, watching us playfully.

Sawyer glared at his cousin before turning back to me. "What's your name there?"

Oh my God, was he going to look at my pictures? That felt…weird. Even though my profile was public and I obviously had followers who looked at them…

"WolfGirl underscore four."

He dipped his head, then popped a final piece of food into his mouth. "I'll see you tonight. At the gala?" He looked longingly at me and I nodded, swallowing hard.

He got up and left and the line of girls frowned, looking at Sage and I with death glares.

"Holy sexual chemistry, Batman!" Sage stared at me wide-eyed. "My cousin *totally* likes you."

I shook my head. "Please, he was just being nice."

My phone dinged and I looked down, my heart leaping into my throat.

WolfDude_4 is following you.

My eyes widened at the name, a direct opposite of mine.

With a shaky hand, I clicked on the profile. He had one picture. A grin spread across my face when I saw the white sneakers under the cafeteria table, ankles crossed. My sneakers. He snuck a picture of my shoes when I wasn't looking and made a profile on Instagram just to follow me.

My mouth went dry when I realized that Sawyer might actually like me and that I might really be in the running for *Werewolf Bachelor*. Against all these perfect preppy dolls...

"I've never seen him like this." Sage startled me and I didn't realize she was looking over my shoulder.

I closed the app, and shrugged. "He had to make a profile in order to see my portfolio. Maybe he likes photography."

She grinned. "First of all, your profile is public, you don't need to make an account to see it. Secondly, he's premed, he loves science and numbers and thinks art is a waste of time."

Ouch, I might have to change his mind on that. Before I could dwell on it further, my tablet started to ding, one chime after another; like an alarm, it kept beeping.

I scrambled to get it out of my bag. "What's that?"

"Oh, it's an alert. They won't stop until you've read it and accept." Sage looked over my shoulder as I pulled the tablet out and read the screen.

"Demi Calloway. Your major has been changed to Advanced Photography. Business has been dropped."

Shock ripped through me...

Sage grinned. "Holy shit."

Sawyer changed my major...

He knew I wouldn't be good wife material with this major and he changed it anyway, knowing I loved it. I wasn't sure if that was a good thing or a bad thing. I wasn't sure of anything anymore.

CHAPTER FIVE

MY FIRST TWO CLASSES WERE AMAZING! MY ENTIRE schedule was incredible, actually. I looked down at the tablet and scanned where my third class would be.

Demi Calloway: Advanced Photography Major

1st Period:	Introduction to Studio
2nd Period:	Digital Production and Image Processing
3rd Period:	Photography Basic Design
Lunch	
4th Period:	Conceptual Process and Photographic Expression

<u>5th Period:</u> Intro to Composition

<u>6th Period:</u> Etiquette Class for Ladies

I scowled at the last class. Well, my schedule was almost perfect. Looks like Sawyer couldn't get me out of that one. Heading over to where the map said my basic design class was, I took the time to appreciate the Fine Arts building. It was different than the other sections of campus I'd been in, less modern glass and stainless steel and more rich woods and colorful walls. It was also pretty void of students. I was venturing to guess that not many women took arts majors while in a mating year, which suited me just fine. Not only were most of my classes full of males, so far there were fewer than ten students in each class, which would give me more time to pick the professors' brains.

I stepped into Photography Basic Design with pep in my step. Taking full-time photography classes was pretty much my dream education. Maybe being here wouldn't be so bad after all. I took a seat next to Sean, a new friend, and we chatted about our ideas for the end-of-year showcase project. Obviously, I had forever to plan, but my mind was already churning with ideas. Professor Woods stepped into the room and nodded to the six of us.

He opened his mouth to start the lesson when Sawyer waltzed into the room with an *Intro to Photography* book slung under his arm.

I froze.

The professor looked as shocked as I did. "Mr. Hudson, can I help you?"

Sawyer gave him a cool grin. "I added this class, if that's okay?"

The professor shook himself, swiping through his tablet. "Of course. I didn't know you liked photography."

Sawyer scanned the room, eyes resting on me. "I've taken a sudden interest."

My cheeks warmed, but I tried to play it cool, like he didn't suddenly just become the most romantic man that ever existed.

He walked to the back of the room and took the seat behind me while my heart hammered in my throat.

Be cool. Maybe he really *does* like photography.

The professor turned to start lecturing on the board, then Sawyer's hand slipped a note onto my desk.

How very 1990. If he didn't do social media, he probably didn't know you could message in Insta, and we hadn't exchanged phone numbers yet.

I tried to keep the grin off my face as I peeled open the note.

We need to talk about last night. Maybe after the gala?

-Sawyer

My stomach sank. And here I was hoping he'd let that go. Was that why he joined this class, to babysit me? To send me covert notes and make sure no one knew my freaky secret? I nodded in case he was watching for a reaction, and then sank into my seat for the rest of the hour.

I watched the clock like a hawk. I just wanted to be out of this class, away from Sawyer's eyes on the back of my neck. I felt...like something was wrong with me, like I should be ashamed of what happened last night, and I just wanted to disappear. The clock was about to strike 12:05, signaling the end of the hour, when a deep loud siren blared down the hallway and a light that I hadn't realized was over the doorway started to flash red.

Stupid fire alar—

Before I could process what was happening, Sawyer yanked me from my seat, tucking me into his chest, as Eugene burst into the room. Brandon and Walsh were right behind him, armed to the teeth.

"Sawyer, code *red*," Eugene said, and I peered up at Sawyer from where I was smooshed to his chest to see the color drain from his face. Everything happened so quickly then; Sawyer moved with the speed of a leopard, darting across the room, dragging me firmly along with him.

"What's happening? What's code red?" I asked as we burst out into the hallway.

Sawyer spun, looking down on me with yellow

eyes, hands grasped protectively around my shoulders. "Vampires."

His warm breath washed over me at the same time terror struck my heart.

Vampires? It had been six years since my attack, but the thought of seeing those death walkers again made my fight-or-flight instinct kick in.

Brandon handed Sawyer a leg harness with three silver stakes, which he clipped onto his thigh.

"Can I have one?" I asked.

Sawyer paused a second, before pulling one of the stakes out and handing it to me.

"So, are we under attack?" My wolf rose to the surface as my canines descended.

Eugene pulled out a large crossbow, loading it with silver arrows. "They'd be stupid to try it."

Sawyer frowned, a low growl ripping from his throat. "If they wanted to talk, they'd have called."

The double doors at the end of the hall opened and I felt alpha power wash over me as Curt Hudson strode down the hallway with two dozen guards at his back.

"Hello, son." He looked at Sawyer and then at me, eyes widening a little. "You look just like your mother," he breathed.

Whoa. I'd forgotten he knew her. I just gulped, clutching the silver stake in my fist.

"What do they want?" Sawyer asked. "How many

are there?" He rocked on his heels as if ready to go into battle.

The alpha continued to look at me quizzically. "There are only two and they want a private word with our newest student, Demi."

A stone sank in my gut. "Uh...what?" I gulped, blinking rapidly and wondering if I heard him correctly.

Sawyer frowned, looking at me. "How do they know you?"

My heart was beating so loudly in my ears that I barely heard his question. Why the hell did they want to talk to me? The case was closed. I dropped the rape case, and they dropped their murder case. What happened to me was private and I would only share it with people when I saw fit. This was not something I wanted to share with Sawyer or his father right now.

"I dunno," I lied.

Seeming happy with my answer, Sawyer turned to his father. "You can tell them to fuck off. They aren't going near her."

My eyebrows hit my hairline at the same time his father's did.

"Sawyer, you're training to be my replacement, remember?" His voice was stern. "You can't tell diplomats from other cities to fuck off."

Sawyer nodded. "You're right, Father. I'll tell them myself." Then he strode off down the hallway.

I stood there shocked as his father and the two dozen

guards trailed after him. When I made a move to follow, Eugene's hand snaked out and gently grabbed my wrist. "Best to stay out of that one."

Eugene and the rest of Sawyer's guards went after him as I stood there with a silver stake in my hand, completely and totally confused.

Why would the vampires take an interest in me after so long? How did they even know I was here?

I mean, there was the matter of the three dead vampire bodies...

The vampire coven leader had said that it looked like a wolf had attacked them. When my parents threatened to go to the Council of Supernatural Creatures about the rape, they let it go. I should be happy that some savior had crashed into that room when I blacked out and killed three of my four attackers...but all I could think about was the fourth.

Vicon Drake lived on to tell the tale and would inherit the royal crown when he came of age.

Meanwhile, I was left behind to live with my demons, demons he put inside of me.

I couldn't think all through lunch. I didn't want to see Sage, or Sawyer, or anyone, so I used my handy tablet and had food delivered to the library, where I was hiding out. After munching on chicken fingers, truffle fries, and chocolate cake, I went to the rest of my classes, lacking my previous enthusiasm.

Why would the vampires say they wanted to talk to me? How the hell did they know I was here? I mean, they knew my name, so I guess if they kept tabs on the admissions department here they would see that Demi Calloway had enrolled...but why care? Six years had gone by since I'd had to speak to the vampire council about the incident and my coming here wouldn't have changed any of that.

Right?

I'd nearly eaten a hole in my stomach with anxiety by the time the gala rolled around. I'd stayed out all day, avoiding seeing Sage or Sawyer until I absolutely had to. And now that the gala was an hour away, I made my way into the dorm to find a gift box on my doorstep. With a grin, I picked it up and looked at the dry-erase note board that hung on my front door. Sage had scrawled a note.

Knock when you get home.– Sage

I sighed, not wanting her to ask questions about the vampire thing. Hopefully news hadn't spread that they came looking for me. Somehow the alpha and Sawyer didn't strike me as the gossiping type, but still, his guards might...

Reaching out, I knocked on her door and she

yanked it open. "Where the hell have you been?" she questioned.

Before I could answer, her eyes flew to the gift in my arms. "Is that from my cousin?"

I jumped at the topic change. "I think so. Wanna help me open it?"

She nodded and then followed me into my room. "So, I got this new eyeshadow palette that I think would look bomb tonight with that gown you bought. Want me to do your makeup?"

I nodded. "Sure, that would be great."

She frowned as I set the gift on the coffee table.

"Hey, you okay? Was it the vampire thing? I mean, that shook us all up. I haven't heard the war sirens in... forever. It was kind of scary."

Okay...she didn't seem like she knew they were here for me.

I nodded. "Yeah, kinda wild."

She reached out and slung an arm around my shoulders. "Don't worry, they know we change alphas every twenty or so years. They are just messing with Sawyer. Keeping him on his game."

Yeah, that wasn't it at all, but I played along.

She pulled her arm from my shoulders and plucked the note from the top of the box, reading aloud.

"Can you really even call yourself a photographer without a fancy camera? Sawyer."

Camera?

He didn't…

I tore open the box and gasped at the Canon Rebel DSLR. It had four different lenses, a lighting kit and tripod, all in a nice clean black carrying bag.

"Holy shit," I breathed.

This was like…a casual one-thousand-dollar gift. But aside from the money…it was a camera I'd always wanted. Thus far I'd only been taking pictures on my old-ass iPhone with a cracked screen. I bought a set of click-on lenses for it on Amazon for twenty bucks that worked surprisingly well, but this…this was next level.

Sage shook her head. "He's totally smitten."

I snorted. "Look around, I'm living in an episode of *Werewolf Bachelor*. He probably sends all the girls gifts right before the first gala. His calling card."

But even as I said it, I knew it wasn't true.

Sage frowned. "Werewolf what?"

Human TV, they probably didn't watch *The Bachelor*. "Never mind. Help me get dressed, I don't want to be late."

Pushing the drama of the day from my mind, I focused on getting ready for the Welcome Gala.

While Sage curled my hair into an elaborate curled updo, I read the bylaws. Well, not all of them, but the ones that pertained to the mating year.

Bylaw 24.1: The longest an Alpha may rule the pack is twenty-five years.

Bylaw 24.2: When the eldest son of the Alpha gets to

his senior year of college, he enters his mating year, and may not graduate without choosing a mate.

I nearly choked on my own spit. Sawyer had to pick a wife within the next nine months or they wouldn't let him graduate!

Bylaw 24.3: The Alpha's son may not take over the pack until engaged.

Okay, well, that was obvious. It was clear they cared so much about having a mate and marriage.

Bylaw 25.3: The prospective female mate must have no obvious breeding issues. It is also desired that she be a virgin.

Breeding issues?

I scoffed, "That's fucked up."

Sage looked over my shoulder. "Eww, the bylaws. Written like a thousand years ago by my ancestors. They make me cringe to read. They really need to update those things."

Relief washed over me. "So they don't take this stuff seriously?"

"Oh, no, they do. Everyone knows they are outdated, but they go along with it."

I closed the tablet and set it on the table, taking a deep breath.

What the hell was I doing? Getting ready for a party where I would corral like sheep with God knows how many women all for a chance to have something I didn't even want. I didn't want to get married! I was twenty-one. And kids! Holy crap. The bylaws said Sawyer could only be alpha for twenty-five years max. That meant once he took over for his dad, he'd have to start pumping out babies pretty much right away.

I held up a hand for Sage to pause curling my hair. "I don't know if I can do this." I stood and paced to the other side of the room.

I liked him, but so did half the school. This was wild, I'd become my worst nightmare. I was some boy-crazy girl. Why else would I do this?

I liked him.

There, I admitted it to myself. The way he yanked me from my seat today during the vampire attack and tucked me to his chest, it was like he'd instinctually gone into protector mode. The entire school could have been under a zombie level attack and he, the second most important person in Wolf City, had saved me. I was the first item he'd grabbed in a house fire.

He also changed his class from what was no doubt a full schedule of premed classes to have a stupid photography class with me. He bought me a camera because he knew I'd love it, not because it was a flashy gift.

"You okay?" Sage frowned, curling iron in midair as I paced before her.

I sighed. "I like your cousin. I do. It's just...this isn't my thing. Fighting for a guy...it feels icky."

She nodded, setting down the curling iron, and walked over to me.

With a sigh, she looked up at me with a haunted expression. "This summer…for an entire week, right before school started, Sawyer ran away."

My eyes widened. Sawyer didn't seem like a rule breaker to me.

Sage continued. "My uncle went nuts, thought he may have been kidnapped, until he found a note from Sawyer. 'I can't do it,' the note said. It was about his mating year."

My heart tightened in my chest and then skipped a beat. Never for one second did I even think that he might not like this as well.

My mouth dropped open as the story pulled me in. "What happened?"

Sage chewed her lip. "My uncle sent half the pack out to look for him. Brandon, Walsh, and I scoured the entire state until he finally called me on the seventh day and said to come get him."

When I didn't speak, she went on: "He was in an off-grid cabin in Montana. Hadn't shaved, was living off the land. I'd never seen him so depressed, and I've seen him through *a lot* of shit."

"Damn." I couldn't imagine the pressure he must feel to be alpha of the largest pack in the world, to be forced into a set of rules he never signed up for.

"I'll never forget what he said to me when I got there." Sage looked out through my window into the dark woods that lay beyond my dorm.

I leaned forward, my mouth going dry as I hung on her every word. "What did he say?"

Sage chewed at her bottom lip. "This is private family shit, okay? You promise never to tell that I told you this story?"

My heart practically leapt out of my chest with anticipation. "Yes."

Sage nodded. "He looked me right in the eyes and said, 'What if I never find anyone to love me for me?'"

And just like that my heart broke in two. He wasn't worried about finding love...he was worried about *being* loved in return. Being the alpha's rich son, it must have messed with his head. Now he wasn't sure who wanted him for him and not just his status or money.

A tear fell down my cheek and I quickly wiped at it before I straightened. "Okay, we're going to be late. Are you almost done with my hair?"

I made a decision then. Sawyer was a decent fucking guy, the only decent guy I'd met in a long time, and I was going to fight for a chance to date him.

CHAPTER SIX

"This is so fucking weird," I whispered to Sage as we entered the giant ballroom. Five circular tables that sat ten girls each were laid with white linen table-cloths and fancy dinnerware. At the head of the room was one small table, where I assumed Sawyer would sit.

"So weird, but tradition is tradition." She shrugged and snagged two appetizers from a passing waiter. She was wearing a long black cocktail dress with a slit up the thigh, and her red hair was twisted up into a sleek high bun.

"Should you even be here?" I walked to the table with only a few girls at it. I didn't know them, so it seemed safe. "You're related."

She grinned. "I'm a spy. Gonna sniff out the bitches that just want his money."

I grinned as we took a seat. "You're totally here for my moral support, aren't you?"

Sage just winked and handed me a tablet that was on the table.

"What's this?" I hit the home button to turn it on.

Welcome to your compatibility quiz flashed across the screen.

"No way," I groaned.

Sage gave me a full-toothed smile. "My aunt's idea. I heard some of the questions are heinous, but all of the girls have to fill them out."

"Well, we have to check it out." I giggled.

"I thought it was good. Will help him weed out the trash," a voice came from beside me, and I looked up to find Meredith wearing a tight teal dress and glaring down at me.

"Table's full, babe. Sorry." Sage gave Meredith her back and I heard her growl before stalking off. The table was super empty.

"Thank you," I whispered to Sage.

Ignoring what was likely eye daggers being shot into my back, I started the quiz.

I entered my name and the first question popped up.

1. How many children do you want?

Sage burst into laughter. "Wow, going right for the kill."

I chuckled, thinking about the question. It was an open answer so I wrote in, *Twin girls*. Because that's what I'd always wanted.

2. **When you get angry, how do you react? (Please be honest)**

Now it was my turn to laugh.

I wrote *Wolf out* as a joke and went to delete it when Sage hit send.

"Bitch!" I growled playfully.

"Hey, Auntie said to be honest."

3. **What is your idea of a perfect date?**

Video games and pizza, I answered.

Sage nodded. "This makes sense. Your lack of fashion is because you are a closet gamer nerd."

I swatted her away and went to the next question.

4. **Would you sign a prenuptial agreement?**

Holy shit.

Yep, not my money, don't want it.

5. **Would you be happy to let Sawyer be the career-focused one while you stay at home with the children and manage the household?**

A low growl revved in my throat.

"Down, girl. My aunt can be a bit 1950s, but she's cool," Sage assured me.

Hell no, I answered, and pressed the button with more force than needed.

Sage winced. "I could have finessed that answer a bit for you."

6. Last question, why are you here?

She probably was looking for me to say, "To find true love" or some shit like that, but that wasn't true. I mean yeah, I wanted to see what this whole "fight for the alpha's son thing" was all about, but truly I was here because Sawyer asked me to be, because there was a spark there, an undeniable attraction and I wanted to see it through.

Because...I wanted to be free.

It was an honest answer but wasn't the full truth. So I added one more line.

And good guys are in short supply, and Sawyer seems to be one of the good ones.

I hit enter and a thank-you note popped up just in time for the entire room to quiet as the lights dimmed.

"Very theatrical," Sage muttered.

The room got eerily dark before lighting up again, and then the alpha and a woman who I assumed was Sawyer's mother entered the room. The girls burst into applause and so did I. I didn't know his parents would be here tonight.

Weird.

I mean, weirder than trying to date a dude with fifty other girls? Guess not.

His mother, a tall and stunningly beautiful woman with long, dark brown hair, stepped up to a podium.

"Hello, ladies." She smiled, her voice sweet and soft.

The girls all clapped again and she blushed. "Sawyer is just looking over the compatibility quizzes you all filled out and then he will join us shortly."

My eyes widened. *Sawyer* was going to look those over? Yikes. Okay. That was fine. I mean, that was good actually, better than his mother.

"I know from my own experience this can all be a bit weird." She looked at the alpha, who gave her a wink, causing heat to creep up her cheeks.

Okay, they were kind of adorable.

"But the rules are the rules and Sawyer cannot lead without a strong, loving woman by his side."

The thunderous applause went up again and I found myself clapping along. I mean, when she put it that way...

The side door opened and then Sawyer entered, and holy hell he was wearing a three-piece suit and looked absolutely sexy as sin. The girls clapped like crazy while I just stared, trying not to drool on my dress.

"All right, well, have fun getting to know Sawyer," his mom said, and left the podium.

The moment the girls started clapping and hollering, Sawyer's body language shut down. His eyes hit the floor, his shoulders drooped, and he looked majorly uncomfortable.

Eugene and some of his security guards flanked the room, standing up against the walls as Sawyer made his way to the front.

I recognized Walsh, Quan, and Brandon from my creepy kidnapper van ride. "So, are they like training to be security? Is that an academic major here?" I eyed the boys.

Sage nodded. "Advanced Techniques in Alpha Security. By the time we graduate, Walsh, Quan, Brandon and I will be the lead guards for Sawyer, his wife, and any children they have."

Holy shit...I had been kidding.

I snort-laughed. "Advanced Techniques in Alpha Security! It's a *major*?" I couldn't get over this, it was too wild. I mean, the witches had Advanced Techniques in Potion Making, but this was somehow funnier to me.

The grin wiped off Sage's face, and she leaned in closer to me. "When Sawyer was a child...he was kidnapped."

My eyes widened. "By who?"

Sage looked left and right to make sure we weren't overheard. "The Paladins, a rogue pack."

Chills ran the length of my arms. "The who?"

She tucked a single stray lock of red hair behind her ear. "A pack that lives just outside the border of Wolf City, in the Wild Lands. They're all feral and unsophisticated. They've always wanted to be alpha, and they claim to have alpha blood in their line. Their leader asserts that he should be given the chance to fight for the title."

I gasped softly. "Fight for it? Like…?"

Sage nodded. "To the death. Barbaric, isn't it?"

I tipped my head. "Totally."

Before I could think more about it, all of the girls stood. One by one, they formed a line at Sawyer's small table at the front, walking up to introduce themselves to him…shake his hand, kiss his cheek.

I stayed seated.

"Come on." Sage pulled me up.

"I've already met him," I told her, groaning.

Sage rolled her eyes. "Do you really want him to pick Meredith for his first date?"

Unrestrained jealousy bloomed in my stomach.

"He's picking dates?" I stood and let her lead me into the herd.

Sage pointed to a printed menu I hadn't noticed before. Underneath all the yummy food listed, it said:

Sawyer will have five mini ten-minute dates join him for dinner based on your compatibility quiz answers.

Ten minutes! Wow, these chicks were desperate for

any time with him. The line was painfully long, and I found myself staring at the yummy steaming trays of food that had been brought in.

"What are you going to say to him so he will pick you for one of the dates?" Sage whispered as Meredith walked up to his table, leaned over so that her tits were in his face, and kissed his cheek.

I blew air through my teeth. "I dunno, I'm thinking maybe I don't want him to pick me so I have more time to eat."

Sage snort-laughed. "Say *that*. He'll love it."

I rolled my eyes and then it was my turn. Sage jumped in front of me and whispered something in his ear, before reaching out and messing up his hair. He grinned at her retreating back, before smoothing his hair, then his eyes fell on me and his whole face went slack.

My mouth went dry as his gaze raked over my tight red dress and he stood, stepping out from behind the table. He took two steps, closing the distance between us, and placed a hand on my lower back as he pulled me in for a hug.

Oh my shifter, he smelled so good. I swallowed hard as his arms came around me and I felt forty-nine daggers stick into my back as all of the girls were watching. When he pulled away, he gave me a devilish smile. "Do you really like video games or did my cousin tell you to say that?"

I didn't know what he was talking about for a second,

I was so enthralled in him just hugging me like we were old friends. Then I remembered the quiz.

I crossed my arms. "Name the game and I'll smoke your ass."

His gaze went half lidded. "I think you're too good to be true, Wolf Girl. Quick, tell me your flaws so I can temper my excitement."

Wolf Girl wasn't an insult coming from him. On his lips it was an endearing pet name and I kind of loved it.

I grinned. "Is being too beautiful a flaw?"

He chuckled. "Certainly not."

I was obviously joking.

"And I mean, I just love to cook and clean all the time, is that a *bad* thing?"

Another joke, I didn't even know how to boil an egg.

His smile widened. "Oh my mother will love that one. What else?"

I was enjoying the banter until a dark thought slipped into my mind.

Rape.

It happened just like that; when I was having fun or enjoying myself, my little inner demon liked to remind me that I was tainted. What would perfect Sawyer think of me if he knew that a gang of vampires took my virginity? My face fell as I tried to think of another fake flaw, and he noticed, his eyes clouding over and brows drawing together.

"I'm food motivated, so I should probably take my seat. That chicken smells divine."

He nodded, but there was a strain between us. He'd sensed my mood change, and now I felt stupid.

I turned to leave and then remembered something. "Oh, thanks for the camera..." I faced him. "And for changing my major to the one I wanted. That was really sweet."

He gave me a smile, but it wasn't as big as before. Something danced behind his eyes like I was a puzzle and he was trying to figure me out. "You're welcome, Demi." He leaned in and kissed my cheek, sending a warm pulse of heat down my spine as his soft skin brushed against me.

There was no denying we had sexual chemistry. It felt like we were magnets constantly being pulled toward each other. It took a lot of effort to pull myself away from his center of gravity.

Sawyer wasn't the bad boy alpha that I stereotypically thought he would be. He was nice, so damn nice that I wanted to fight all these bitches for him.

When I turned to walk back to my seat, every eye was on me, lips curled and scowls in place.

Oops, my bad.

My gaze flicked to Sage and she was grinning like a fool.

I had just reached my seat when Sawyer handed his mother a piece of paper. Walking over to the podium, she smiled.

"Meredith Pepper, would you please join Sawyer as his first date?"

A sharp pain sliced through my heart and my face fell. Meredith made sure to look back at me with a smirk before she walked up to join Sawyer at his table, her dress tight and clinging to her perfect thin frame.

Sage leaned over. "His mom probably made him pick her first. She's best friends with Meredith's mom."

I put a fake smile on and nodded. "Yeah, whatever."

The waiter set a tray of food down before me and I forgot all about not being picked first. I served myself the smoked chicken with a honey glazed sauce and wild rice with a side of garlic potatoes while the other girls at the table ate salads.

"Is there dessert?" I looked around after eating my second bread roll. Sawyer was on his third date. Spoiler alert: I hadn't been picked yet, but whatever, we were just friends. He brought me here to save me from Delphi hell, not to date me. I was already over it.

Sage snorted. "Menu says low-calorie gelato, but I know the chef and we can request chocolate cake if you want."

I rolled my eyes. "As if that is even a question. I want!"

She got up and went to speak to the waiter while I watched Sawyer talk to Priya. He looked bored but she was insanely gorgeous, so how bored could he *really* be?

Ten minutes later, I patted my food baby as I licked the chocolate off my fork. "Holy yum."

"You haven't started the etiquette classes yet, have

you?" Sage observed as she neatly cut a piece of chocolate cake before sticking it into her mouth.

"Hey." I punched her arm playfully.

"Is Demi Calloway here?" Sawyer's mother's voice called loudly from the front of the stage.

Shit. I wiped the last vestiges of chocolate from my mouth as my attention snapped to the front and I stood, heart beating in my chest.

"You are Sawyer's last date of the evening." She gave me a sweet smile, but I could tell she didn't look thrilled about her son choosing me. I was regretting the "Hell no" comment on my compatibility form right about now. As I walked up to the front of the room, Sawyer's gaze tracked me like he was stalking his prey, face void of any emotion, so I couldn't read what he was thinking. When I reached the table, he stood and pulled out my chair like one of those fancy guys in movies.

Maybe I *did* need the etiquette classes.

I took a seat and he slipped in next to me, moving his chair closer. "You smell like chocolate," he whispered, causing a grin to pull at my lips.

"While you were enjoying your low-calorie gelato, Sage snagged us the good stuff."

Another grin pulled at his lips and my entire stomach dropped out. Sawyer was one of those guys who got hotter when they smiled, like a rare gift you weren't prepared for. And *bam,* it came out of nowhere.

"I think I have the good stuff right here." He winked at me.

Holy shifter babies, it took me a second to realize he was talking about me. Maybe we weren't just friends...

I gulped and gave a nervous laugh. "Yeah, you totally pick the *good stuff* last," I jived. "Makes perfect sense."

He leaned in, bringing the heat of his body with him. "I saved the *best* for last. That way we can sneak out of here and no one will expect to see me anymore."

I froze as a devilish smile played at my lips. "Sneak out?"

He nodded, calmly looking at his mother and father, who sat off to the side. He gave them a little wave. "That way we can go on a *real* date."

My heart jumped wildly in my chest at his proclamation. I remembered the note he passed to me in photography class; maybe he also wanted to talk about that. "What's your plan to escape the royal entourage, my liege?" I gestured to the crowd and he smiled.

"Well, my lady, I was thinking first you should give me a kiss on the cheek. You know, for theatrical reasons."

"Of course," I agreed.

"And then walk away from the table and go outside. I will say good night to everyone and meet you outside the back entrance." He cracked his knuckles like it was the perfect plan.

I couldn't help the stupid boy-crazy smile that lit up my face.

"I accept this mission," I told him.

Leaning in, I kissed his cheek, letting my lips stay there longer than was probably appropriate, and then stood from the table and gave a big fake yawn. "Good night, Sawyer. I'm tired."

He gave me a halfcocked smirk. "Night, Demi." Then he winked as I walked away from the table. When I got to the back of the room, I walked toward the exit doors at the left, away from Sage, who was waiting for me. She looked confused, and then grinned. She must have put together what we were doing. Pushing the doors open, I hit the fresh night air just as I heard Sawyer wish everyone a good night.

Creeping around the side of the building in my heels, I found the back entrance. Eugene was waiting there but he didn't look confused at my approach. "Good evening, Miss Calloway."

I swallowed. "Hi. Good evening. Er, Sawyer asked me—"

The doors opened and Sawyer walked outside, casually slipping his hand into mine, and butterflies took flight in my stomach. We started to walk down a dark moonlit corridor and headed toward a building I didn't recognize.

"Did they buy it?" I whispered, leaning into his shoulder, loving the way it felt to touch him, to hold his hand and be close to his body.

Sawyer shook his head. "Meredith looked suspicious, and Mother gave me quite the scowl."

Laughter pealed out of me. "Oh no. Not a *scowl.*"

"Sawyer!" Meredith's voice stretched into the night air and we both simultaneously burst into a run, trying to contain our laughter. Running down the hallway, escaping his ex-girlfriend and laughing about it was a highlight of my night.

After a moment, I glanced over my shoulder and I saw Eugene walking briskly behind us but not Meredith.

Whew. Crisis averted.

When we reached a stone arch doorway to what I assumed was his house, we were both panting and out of breath. One of my curls was stuck to my lip gloss, jostled from the run. Reaching out, he tenderly brushed the hair away from my lips.

"So, how are you going to win me over?" I asked. "This better be the best date of my life, because I have a lot of prospects you know." I gestured to the empty dark night.

A slow grin pulled at his lips. "I like you, Demi. You're not like the others."

The *others.* And just like that he reminded me that I was in a race to win his heart with forty-nine women of various shapes, sizes, and colors.

Gross.

"I was thinking pizza and video games." He opened the door to the room and I took in the scene before me with a grin.

He must have had someone set this up while we were

eating. The space opened up into a small but luxurious apartment, very modern and masculine. On the coffee table was a pizza takeout box, and around it were various video game cases and two controllers.

I couldn't stop smiling; my cheeks actually hurt.

I spied a game I was exceptionally good at as I stepped into the apartment. "Is that *Call of Duty*?"

He winced. "Too gory for a first date?"

I chuckled. "I think I'll be fi—"

My brag was cut off by a hissing sound, and that's when the coppery scent of vampire stench hit my nose. Someone reached out from behind the dark hallway and grasped my shoulders, sending panic flying through me.

"Eugene!" Sawyer yelled into the courtyard and then burst forward, yanking me by the wrists and wrestling me out of my attacker's grip. In one quick move, Sawyer tucked me behind him, and then I heard the cracking of bones. But the vampire moved blindingly fast, plowing into Sawyer's half-shifted form while I watched in horror as they collided.

My wolf clawed at the surface of my skin as I longed to help Sawyer fight him off, but he'd told me not to shift in front of anyone but him...Eugene burst through the door, two silver stakes in hand, and that's when four other vampires stepped out from the shadows.

Shit.

They were all male, more muscular than the royalty I was accustomed to seeing around Delphi when they came for visits or threw parties. These men were warriors, hired assassins.

"Demi, run!" Eugene shouted, and then turned into a badass assassin. He was a blur of motion as he attacked the oncoming horde of vampires, but I knew from experience they were just too damned fast. Sawyer was in the hallway tearing into the first vamp if those screams were any indication, while Eugene tried to fight off the others.

I backed up into the kitchen, grabbing the first knife handle out of the wooden block by the stove that I could reach.

Please don't be that useless sharpener stick.

In a blur of motion, one of the vampires had reached me and I looked down, relief coursing through me at the giant twelve-inch blade in my hand.

The vampire inhaled through his nose, like he was smelling me. "I found her!" he shouted behind him to the others, and my stomach dropped.

What?

My wolf rattled against my ribs like a cage. I was so used to keeping her inside, but I wasn't sure I could do that now, not in a life-or-death situation like this. I knew Sawyer had told me never to let anyone see me shift but maybe that weird split shift thing was a one-time freak accident?

Before I could think any more on it, the vampire lunged for me and I got stabby.

After my sexual assault, I had a hard time sleeping—being a boring old human was such a helpless feeling in a world full of magical creatures. Although I wasn't *just* a boring human, with my cuffs I might as well have been. A week after the attack, I signed up for self-defense classes and slept soundly that night for the first time in days. They weren't just any self-defense classes. The class was taught by a badass named Krev who had been with the Israeli special forces. If I was going to live my whole life without shifting, I needed to turn my body into a weapon. I still had years of training to become a total badass, but I knew enough to hopefully not stab myself with this knife in a fight.

The vampire went right for my throat and I tracked the motion, keeping my grip firm on the knife as I lashed out quickly and stabbed him right in the armpit. He hissed, kicking out, but I saw it coming and jumped up and over it. In human form I was faster than a normal human, but not as fast as a vampire. I wouldn't be able to outrun one, but I should be able to stay alive…I hoped.

"Do you even know what you are?" he hissed, his gelled black hair having come undone in our scuffle.

His question was causing panic to creep up my throat as I assessed the situation around me. Eugene had killed two vampires and was still in human form; Sawyer was bounding down the hall, black ashy blood around his muzzle. So that left just this one and possibly one other.

Everything is going to be fine.

I'd just keep him talking and Sawyer would rip his head off in a moment.

"I'm a contestant in *Werewolf Bachelor*," I told him, thinking of the first thing I could and causing his brows to knit together in confusion. I took that moment of confusion and lashed out again, this time aiming for the kill zone, right over his unbeating heart. I got three short stabs in while he staggered backward.

Thump, thump, thump.

My eyes widened as I heard someone running across the roof.

The vampire grinned, right before Sawyer leapt into the air and took his head clean off. His powerful wolf's jaws clamped down over the vampire's neck and ripped his head from his body, causing it to wither and turn to an ashy lump. Eugene relaxed the slightest bit, scouting the area with his eyes for any more attackers when I felt it.

The hairs raised on my arms and a sense of impending doom took over me.

"There's more." I barely got the words out before the windows crashed inward and everything happened so quickly I could barely process it.

Sawyer stepped over the vampire's headless withering body to tuck himself into my leg and Eugene started to shift, bones cracking and his form bulking out in record speed. Six vampires had just broken through the windows of Sawyer's living room, and there was a familiar whirring sound outside, making its way over to us.

Helicopter.

This wasn't some little mission to mess with the alpha's son, this was a carefully planned operation.

The entire thirty seconds I processed this felt like two hours, like time had slowed and I was out of my body. It took me a moment to realize, I *was* out of body. A white, ghostly wolf form *crawled* out of my body, leaving my clothes unmarred. Pain ripped across my skin as my wolf left me, and then she solidified, no longer spectral as she stood next to Sawyer and growled at the oncoming horde.

What the hell? This time wasn't like last time, I hadn't even gone furry, she'd just...detached from me and solidified like a ghost coming back to life.

Eugene's wolf had shifted as well and he was insanely huge, two times the size of mine and bigger than Sawyer's by a long shot, but he was frozen, staring at me as he'd just witnessed my freak of nature.

"It's her! She's the one!" a female vampire wearing black army fatigues hissed from the living room.

The other vampires had come in to weaken or distract, or maybe to confirm something.

Me. To confirm it was me that they wanted for whatever reason.

These vampires were here to kill. They held sleek black guns that I just knew were full of silver bullets.

Kill me? Kill Sawyer and take me? I didn't want to know the answer to that question.

Sawyer's wolf looked mine in the eyes and I felt a pressure in my skull, alpha power pressed in on me like a blanket.

'Run. Get help,' his voice projected into my mind and my eyes widened.

I knew that the alpha had powers the other wolves didn't; it was in their bloodline, like a magic none of us had, but I didn't know the extent of those powers. I was scared to leave him, scared that if I did he might die and I'd never get that first date. I shook my head and my wolf tipped her head back and let loose with a long, haunting howl. Eugene and Sawyer joined in, until our howls became deafening.

Hopefully, one of the guards on campus heard that and would come to investigate, because we were out of time. Two of the vampires raised their guns, aiming them at Eugene and Sawyer, and I didn't know what I was thinking, but I burst forward to stand in the line of fire.

Simultaneously, my wolf and my human form lurched forward, throwing ourselves in front of the boys and in front of two oncoming bullets. Time was weird. I could see the bullets flying through the air in slow motion like I was in an action movie. It took me a second to realize time hadn't slowed, but I'd sped up.

I was fast, *vampire-fast.*

Thrusting my hands out, I caught the bullets as they tore through the flesh in my palms. Sharp burning pain sliced through my palms as the bullets exited the back of my hands and landed on the floor. A high-pitched scream of agony ripped from my throat.

My wolf was already taking one of the vampires down, while the other vampire stared at me in shock.

"She moved like us," the male bloodsucker said stupidly.

"Get her before she grows too strong!" the female vampire snapped, and they all advanced in unison. I was experiencing my wolf tearing into the vampire closest to me while also staring down at the two holes in my hands. It's like wherever I willed my attention to go, it went, but each body could think and act independently of the other. The holes seeped crimson, blending in with the red color of my pretty dress as I fought the very strong urge to have a mental breakdown.

What the fuck was happening? Why couldn't I just be eating pizza or making out right now?

Something bumped into my leg and I yelped, only to find it was Sawyer's dark gray wolf. He pushed me behind him as he and Eugene curled their lips back and growled at the vampires before us.

I was staring at my hands in fascination where the holes seemed to be getting smaller, while simultaneously feeling my wolf kill the vampire. I could see his screaming face, taste his putrid blood, but I was also just standing here staring at my hands.

Was I losing my mind? Was this really happening?

In unison, Eugene and Sawyer leapt, taking two vampires down to the ground each, leaving only the female. She took one look at my wolf, standing on the dead body of her friend, and hissed, retreating out the broken back window and into the night.

Helicopter blades whirred, and then only the sound of Eugene and Sawyer tearing into the flesh of the undead remained.

Howls rose into the night and Sawyer froze, looking at my wolf.

'Shift back. Now.'

My heart hammered in my throat as my wolf bounded over to me. I stood there stupidly, staring at the weeping holes in my hands, which were nearly closed. Werewolves had rapid healing but not *this* rapid, and *not* when silver was involved. I should be in surgery right now…I should be…

I gasped as my wolf jumped into the air, headed right for me. Tensing, I flexed my muscles, preparing for her to slam into me. The hit never came, because right before she reached me, she went semitransparent and was sucked inside of me. There was pressure, slight pain, and then it was gone.

"What the *fuck* was that!" Eugene stood, naked and holding his junk as he stared at me, wide-eyed.

Sawyer walked across the room and I totally shamelessly checked out his amazing naked ass. He opened a linen closet and slipped on some basketball shorts. When he returned, he gave Eugene a large blanket. I was assuming because no shorts of his would fit the giant man.

"That was an assassination attempt," Sawyer told him as Eugene wrapped the blanket around his waist like a towel.

Eugene shook his head. "No. *Her*."

Sawyer stepped closer to the head of security. "*That* was an assassination attempt."

Eugene's eyes widened. "Sawyer, I work for your father. I have to tell him about her—"

"You protect *me*! Next year you will work for *me*."

Conflict warred in Eugene's gaze and he looked from me and back to Sawyer.

"Please," Sawyer begged. "Don't tell him about Demi."

Eugene's eyes widened and the sound of footsteps drew nearer.

"Why not?" Eugene whispered.

Silence descended over the room as Sawyer weighed his answer, before looking over at me sadly.

He lowered his voice to barely a whisper: "Because my father will have her killed."

Fear trickled into my bones at his declaration, and then the footsteps arrived. Twenty armed Wolf City guards burst into Sawyer's apartment, eyes wide.

Eugene took a deep breath and held the blanket firmly around him. "Please inform the alpha there has been an assassination attempt by the vampire coven. I'll want to do a full investigation."

Somewhere in the past few minutes, I'd started crying. I was still staring at my hands, now fully healed, as tears splashed down on them.

Sawyer's bare feet came into view and he reached down and picked me up, scooping me under the knees and holding me tightly to his chest. "I'm taking her to the hospital to get checked out," Sawyer informed the men present.

"I'll take her, sir." One of them reached for me and Sawyer growled, low and deep in his throat, causing the man to back up several steps until he bumped into the wall.

He walked me out the front door and I couldn't stop crying, the tears tracing tracks down my cheeks and onto his bare chest.

What was wrong with me? What the hell was that back there? I moved like a vampire, I fought alongside my wolf, my hands healed in seconds!

"I'm scared," I whimpered, no longer caring about acting cool in front of Sawyer. Whatever dreams I had of this man picking me as his wife and mate were dashed when I fucking caught bullets midair like a freak.

He looked down at me, conflicted emotions warring in his face. "Me too," he finally said, and it was not what I wanted to hear.

Not at all.

CHAPTER SEVEN

"SO, FIRST DATE WAS A LITTLE BUST, NO BIGGIE." SAGE sat at my bedside in the hospital, which, surprise, was called Hudson Emergency Room. It seemed his family owned everything in Werewolf City. Everything important anyway.

I snorted. "A little bust? We all nearly *died*."

What a horrible first date. Sawyer was clearly never going to speak to me again. Because of me, he had threatened Eugene and lied to his father. This was so fucked, and it sucked because I really liked him.

Sage shrugged. "I mean, if you want to be the alpha's wife, you need to be used to attacks."

I didn't respond, because this wasn't an attack for the alpha's son, it was for me, but I hadn't told her that.

"I just want to go home."

She nodded. "I'll have the nurse get your discharge papers."

I'd been found to have no wounds, but Sawyer had told the doctor to keep me for a few hours to make sure I remained stable. I think he feared for my mental health more than anything. Which right now was teetering on the brink.

When Sage returned a few moments later with a stack of papers, I sighed in relief. I just wanted to go back to my dorm, take a hot shower, and forget this shit show ever happened.

We made our way outside, where a sleek black car was waiting.

"I didn't think you would want to ride a scooter across campus looking like Carrie on Halloween," Sage informed me.

I looked down at my crusted bloody red dress and gave her a wry smile. "Very thoughtful of you."

It was a five-minute ride across campus to our dorm, and because of the late hour we were able to slip in undetected. Even the front door lady, a different one than Kendra this time, was asleep at the desk. I did notice, though, that the campus was crawling with security.

Sage dropped me off at my front door. "Get some sleep. I'll be right out here if you need anything."

I frowned.

She grinned. "I've been assigned as your own personal bodyguard."

I gave her a wan smile, but it didn't feel real. Neither she, nor I, knew what she was guarding.

I wasn't a normal werewolf, that was for damn sure.

It was a long time before I could fall asleep.

The next day, I threw on black yoga pants and a t-shirt that said *Classy but I cuss a little*. After tossing my hair into a top knot, I put my camera around my neck and slung my backpack over my shoulder because I gave zero fucks about what I looked like right now. I was just trying to tell myself that yesterday was in the past. Today, I was a photography student and I was going to focus on that.

Something normal.

When I opened the door, Sage was there waiting with two coffees. Her hair was still damp and she wore no makeup but still managed to look incredibly beautiful.

"Did you sleep?" I asked.

She shrugged. "Got four hours while Walsh took over my shift. We're getting new schedules today. There are to be two guards on you at all times."

My eyes bugged and she waved me off. "It's more common once Sawyer picks his top five girls later this year, but you got in early." She winked.

Yeah...I'm not sure that was a good thing.

When we arrived at breakfast, I noticed Sawyer sitting at a table full of girls. One on each side of him and two across from him. Sage and I clutched our trays of food and walked to find a table. "I'll ask them to move," she said, but I shook my head.

"I'd like to just eat alone and get to class," I told her.

Her face fell, but she nodded. "Okay."

We sat as I silently pushed my eggs around the plate. When I looked up, Sawyer glanced over at me, gave me a wan smile and looked away, back to his conversation with Priya and Meredith.

My heart pinched as I came to the realization that things between Sawyer and I were probably over before they began. I had too much baggage for him, and if I was being honest, I wasn't a fan of this whole dating game. I didn't want to share him, I didn't want to feel second best, or third or fiftieth. I wanted to punch all these bitches in the face and then straddle him right in this cafeteria and kiss him in front of everyone.

Sigh.

Brandon and Walsh walked up, fully outfitted for war, with knifes, stakes, and guns strapped over their black canvas jumpsuits. Every eye in the cafeteria tracked their movements.

Don't come over here, don't come over here.

They stopped at our table. "Demi, we will be accompanying you to your classes today," Brandon told me.

Great.

I chugged my OJ and grabbed my stuff. "I'll see you at lunch," I told Sage, and stood, following them out of the cafeteria. I risked a glance behind me, just in time to see Sawyer look up at me and then turn away quickly.

My first two classes were agony. All I could think about was what I would say to Sawyer in my third period class. I wanted to apologize for any inconvenience this whole vampire attack thing caused him, because clearly it was my fault. I wanted to tell him I was still down to play *Call of Duty* anytime he wanted. I wanted shit to feel normal between us because we'd started something fresh and real and exciting, and I didn't want to lose it. By the time the bell rang for third period, I was already in my desk, eyeing the door and waiting for him to walk through.

But he never did...

The seconds stretched to minutes, which turned into the full hour, and my heart sank.

He'd dropped the class.

He was so freaked about last night that he didn't want to pursue me anymore.

Could I blame him?

I'd nearly gotten him killed. I was some human-wolf split shifter. I caught bullets, and I made him lie to his dad.

Future wife material.

By the time it was lunch hour, I felt sick to my

stomach. I missed my best friend Raven and my parents. I actually sort of missed Delphi at this point. At least things there were predictable. I didn't want to go to the cafeteria and see all of the women fawn all over Sawyer, so I decided to linger in the park for a bit. Walsh and Brandon were following me at a twenty-foot distance, but I could feel them just staring at me, waiting for a vampire to jump out and attack me or something.

With a sigh, I texted Sage.

Me: Want to eat outside today?

Sage: Yep, I'll bring you carb-loaded, fattening, high-calorie food?

I grinned.

Me: Yes please. Meet you at the park.

I was about to put my phone away when it binged. The Sterling Hill app I had downloaded had a notification. I opened it and my heart leapt into my throat.

Dear Mating selection candidate,

Starting tomorrow, Sawyer will be picking two dates per day, one for lunch and one for dinner. He will do this each day of the week for the next month until he has had time to personally meet with each one of you one-on-one. At the end of the month, you will be informed if he has invited you to continue with the mating selection process and move into the top twenty chosen. Please be ready each day for a date in case you are chosen, as these things can be last minute.

Have a wonderful day,

Mrs. Hudson

Fuck that. Be ready every single day for a month in case he chose me? This whole thing was starting to make me sick and pissed off. I growled and stomped into the park. I would be a lot more frustrated if this damn garden wasn't so beautiful. A stunning pink bougainvillea had caught my eye. The way it curved over the stone arch entryway of the park and how the light filtered through it was enchanting. I *had* to get a picture. Pulling out my phone, I stood under the hulking lush flowers and tipped my head up to snap a photo. Only afterward did I realize I now had a fancy camera.

Slipping my phone into my back pocket, I pulled out the camera Sawyer had bought me, messing with the settings until I got what I wanted. I was on my fourth picture when my phone buzzed in my back pocket.

WolfDude_4 has uploaded a new photo.

I clicked the alert, fully prepared for a selfie or even a picture with Meredith.

When I saw the back of *me*, taking a picture of the pink flowers moments ago with my phone, I gasped and spun around the park searching for him, but he was nowhere.

My heart pounded in my throat as I read the caption. It was…a poem?

"Some days, I am more wolf than woman and I am still learning how to stop apologizing for my wild" —*Wolf and Woman* by Nikita Gill.

What the hell, he knew poetry? And what did that mean? That I shouldn't be sorry for who I was?

"Hey." Sage called, bringing my attention back to reality and I jumped a little.

"Hey." I quickly *"liked"* the photo, and then slipped my phone back away and into my pocket.

Sage handed me a plate of chicken fingers and French fries with extra ranch and I grinned.

"Thanks."

We sat on a bench and Sage popped a fry into her mouth. "So the rumor mill is in full effect."

I raised an eyebrow. "Oh?"

She nodded. "Some people saw you and Sawyer go back to his place last night. Then they heard about the vampire attack. You're a banished wolf." She gave me a sly grin. "So naturally everyone thinks you are really in league with the vampires and are here to assassinate Sawyer."

I gasped and a French fry lodged right into my windpipe. With a huge cough, I was able to spit it out, but it took a moment for me to gather my composure.

"Say what now?" I looked at my redheaded friend.

Sage laughed. "It's ridiculous. No one believes it."

I frowned. "But maybe they do. Maybe the alpha does, ohmygod maybe Sawyer does."

Maybe that's why he dropped the class…? But no, he was there last night, he saw the vampires try to kill me.

I sighed, throwing my head into my hands.

Rumors were powerful, and Sawyer dropping the class he had with me spoke volumes.

I liked him, like I had really allowed myself to like him, and now I felt a little crushed.

Stupid *Werewolf Bachelor*. Not everyone came out of these things happy.

Sawyer would.

Another girl would…

And forty-nine of us would be heartbroken.

Sage waved me off. "Trust me, babe. Everything will blow over by next week."

I wanted to believe her, but I just couldn't.

CHAPTER EIGHT

THAT NIGHT I WAS FULLY PREPARED TO JUST SIT around and eat ice cream all night, but Sage had other plans.

"You just need to dance your way out of your funk. Let's go to Moonies tonight?" she asked.

Moonies was the campus dance club and bar. I'd walked past it a bunch of times and written it off. But I did like to dance…Raven and I took a hip-hop class all through high school that was offered at Delphi and it was something I was good at. Getting lost in the music, moving your body to the beat, there was a therapeutic nature to dancing.

"Maybe for like one dance," I told her, and she squealed.

After dressing me in quite possibly the shortest black dress I'd ever worn, we walked to Moonies with Walsh and Brandon trailing behind us.

“I can’t believe you’re still wearing those fucking white tennis shoes.” She scowled at my feet, causing me to grin.

“First of all, Converse are not tennis shoes. At least I don’t think they are. And second, I can’t believe you care so much about my attire.”

She laughed, hooking her arm through mine and looking over her shoulder at Brandon and Walsh. She’d been doing that a lot lately, sneaking glances at the two men.

I lowered my voice, leaning into her. “Which one do you like?”

Her eyes went wide and she swallowed hard. “Is it that obvious?”

I shrugged. “Just to me.”

She chewed her lip. “Walsh, but he’s Sawyer’s best friend and would never...”

I yanked her arm, pulling her closer to me. “You don’t know that.”

She nodded. “I do. He told me this summer when we kissed.”

Oh. Well, shit.

“Just one kiss? Or was there repeated kissing?” I questioned, raising one eyebrow.

She chuckled. “Just one, amazing, Earth-shattering kiss.”

A frown pulled at my lips. “I’m sorry.”

She gave a casual shrug, but I could see how much it

bothered her. "I'm one of the guys, ya know. Girls like that don't get dated. Anyway, enough about me, did you know that Werewolf City drinking age is eighteen?"

I smiled. "I did. My mom has a really funny story of getting hammered on her eighteenth birthday and my grandma making her sleep it off in the barn with the goats because she kept vomiting."

Sage burst into peals of laughter, but before we could say any more, we'd reached the door. I slipped my hand into my purse, prepared to show ID, when the bouncer just winked at Sage and opened the door.

"Miss Hudson." He nodded, and let us in.

Sometimes I forgot her dad was the alpha's little brother—until someone said her last name.

The flashing lights and deep bass music filtered out to us as we crossed the threshold.

A young woman in her twenties with bright pink hair stood behind a hostess stand and handed us two free drink tickets. "It's ladies' night," she told us with a wink.

Sweet.

I surveyed the club, taking it all in. Moonies was cute, not a huge place; it wasn't sure whether it wanted to be a college bar or a high-tech dance club, but it had a special something, a vibe. The walls were all, surprise, glass, and the floors were stamped concrete, but the bar which took up the entire right side of the space was deep rich wood and had stacks of schoolbooks in shelves near the ceiling as decoration. I kind of dug it. I was scanning for two seats at the bar since the place was packed, when my gaze landed on two searing blue eyes.

Fuck.

"Sawyer's here," I mumbled to Sage. "Let's go." I yanked her arm.

"I can't hear you!" she shouted over the loud music.

I couldn't take my eyes off of his, he was just...watching me, drinking me in while a familiar blond hung on his arm, talking to her friends.

Darth Vader.

Oh my God, was this their date night? Of course he chose her first.

"Shit, Sawyer's here with Meredith!" Sage screamed into my ear and I nodded.

Sawyer stood, shaking Meredith off of his arm as she continued to talk to her friends, and he just...stared at me.

"Who goes to a bar for a date?" I yelled in Sage's ear.

She grinned. "Meredith. She's a lush who loves attention. This is like her favorite place."

"We should go!" I told Sage, yanking her arm again.

She pulled me on the dance floor with surprising force, ignoring my plea. "Don't worry! He's faking that he is into all these girls because he has to. *Trust me*," Sage said.

She had no idea. No idea what went down with the vamps, and no idea what I was or that he'd dropped his class to escape me.

Fuck it.

Sage was right. Screw planning my every minute around Sawyer. I was here to have fun and I wasn't going to let him being on a date with another chick bother me. Turning my back to him, I started to dance. I mean, full-on pelvic thrusting, rolling my body with the music as I threw my arms up in the air to music and let my hair whip around.

"Yes, girl!" Sage screamed in laughter as I gestured to her and shook my boobs at her, causing her to laugh. Dancing with girlfriends was always the best because you didn't have to worry about them hitting on you, and you didn't have to worry about being an idiot. I just let go of everything, let go of what I might be, of Sawyer, of all my stress. I moved my body to the music and owned that dance floor, rubbing up against Sage with my butt as she smacked it and laughed.

Zero. Fucks. Given.

A bunch of guys had started to form a circle around us, cheering us on and ogling like the stupid assholes they were, but we didn't care, we just kept on dancing. This music was my jam and I was living my best life.

When I spun in the air, I risked a glance behind me, searching for Sawyer, and my wolf rose to the surface when I noticed two yellow eyes standing twelve inches from me.

I skidded to a stop, heart pounding in my chest either

from dancing or the fact that Sawyer was a mere foot away from me.

"Uh…hey," I huffed, panting.

He blinked, eyes flashing from yellow to blue. His gaze flicked to the guys standing in a circle watching us and his jaw clenched. He leaned into me, pressing a hand at my lower back and pulling me into him. When his lips grazed my ear, heat traveled down my spine and settled between my legs. "Please go home," he said. "Don't make me rip their eyes out." He gestured to the men who were now watching Sage dance.

My blood went cold.

Sawyer Hudson was jealous. I would smile, but there was no humor in his voice and I thought he might actually be serious. Alpha males were known for being territorial with women they were dating, but this was next level. I couldn't even be looked at? Just because I was one of fifty women he was dating?

Anger flared inside of me and I pulled away from him. "Why did you drop photography?" I yelled.

Regret crossed his face. "My mother made me. Said it would interfere with getting into med school." He looked embarrassed and I actually laughed at that a little.

"Future alpha lets his mom tell him what classes to take?" I winked playfully.

He normally liked my humor, but right now he wasn't smiling, he was watching the men in the circle around us and then looking back at my dress, his gaze bouncing to my thighs, my cleavage, my neck. His eyes flashed yellow again and he pressed in on me one more time.

"Please...go home, Demi." His voice was thick with his wolf and I frowned, crossing my arms in defiance.

"Why?"

He took a deep breath, leaning into my ear, his lip caressing the lobe. "Because you're *mine*, and if I have to watch these guys look like they want to fuck you any longer, I will lose my mind."

Shock ripped through me.

You're mine.

Okay, that was normally such an annoying male wolf thing to say, but on Sawyer's lips it was hot as fuck.

I swallowed hard and nodded, genuinely afraid he would hurt someone now. His wolf was close, I could smell it.

"Sawyer, what the hell!" Meredith's shrill voice cut into the song and I turned away from him, from her, from all of it. I just grabbed Sage's hand and left the bar more confused than when I'd gotten there.

The next three weeks and six days passed by painfully slow. Sawyer had quite literally gone on a date with every single eligible female here at school but me. I would say he was ignoring me, but every time I saw him he went out of his way to walk over and say hi. When I was eating alone or in the library, he plopped right down next to me and asked how my day was going. He also left comments on all of my Instagram photos and genuinely seemed interested in my art. It was...infuriating. Why couldn't he just be an asshole so I could get over him? Instead, he was traipsing around campus with the entire female school body. Every single girl wore full-on clubbing attire until Sawyer picked them for a date. Then they went back to their regular preppy clothes, which were just a step down from clubbing attire.

Me? Oh, I'd had Raven mail me my prized custom t-shirt collection, and currently I was wearing *Single but not interested.* It matched my fishnets and jean shorts look.

I didn't give a fuck anymore. Sawyer could pick me tonight for dinner, as it was the last slot open, and I wouldn't even change. That's how much I didn't care. But seeing as though it was 4:30pm and I was in the developing lab, processing my negatives, I might not even say yes. I clipped the 8x10 pictures I'd taken of Sage up on the drying line with more force than was necessary and checked my phone for the twentieth time.

Obviously it was too late! He was going to skip over me like an asshole and cut me from the top twenty without even giving me a chance.

What a hot and cold asshole. One second he's all possessive and the next he isn't into me.

I was so mad, I barely registered the knock at the door.

"Room's taken!" I growled.

They knocked again.

Ugh. Taking off my apron, I crossed the room and pulled the blackout curtains closed before opening the door.

My tongue went dry when I saw Sawyer holding a dozen red roses and wearing a black suit and tie.

"Hey," I said stupidly.

His eyes roamed my body, starting at my Doc Martens, up my fishnets and then resting on my shirt, where he grinned.

"I hope that's not a message for me?"

Fuck. Why did I wear this?

I crossed my arms. "Saving the best for last again?" There was more hurt in my voice than I intended and I regretted it, because his playful demeanor changed. Eugene and two other guards I didn't know were at the far end of the hallway waiting for him.

He shook his head, looking at the flowers before handing them to me. "This time it's different."

This time it's different? What the hell did that mean?

I took the flowers as an awkward silence descended upon us.

"Demi?" Sawyer's voice was rough, his eyes hooded.

"Yeah?"

"Would you do me the honor of being my date for dinner tonight?"

He was so serious, and also so charming. Dammit. "Extra carbs, extra gluten?" I raised one eyebrow.

He grinned, and fuck me he had a dimple in his cheek that I didn't realize was there before. "Extra whatever you want." His voice was deep and I'm pretty sure my cheeks went bright red.

I really wanted to say *Whatever I want?* in a sultry voice, but I decided playing hard to get was better.

I looked at my bare wrist, which didn't have a watch on it. "I dunno, I mean it's getting late and you're all dressed up. I'm not sure I have time to get ready."

His eyes flashed yellow for the slightest second as his wolf came to the surface. "I think you look amazing."

Dammit, he was so sweet.

"All right, well, I guess I could run home and change. Where are we going?"

He grinned. "Eugene will bring you. Just be ready by six?"

I nodded and he lingered for a second, looking down at the flowers in my hands. "Are you happy here, Demi? I know it's probably a lot different from Delphi...but my intention was to bring you here for a better life. You're happy, right?" He frowned and I found myself mystified by his genuine goodness.

Ha! Yes, this place was different from the reject magic school. He had no idea. Banishing a wolf was the cruelest thing you could do. Being the only wolf at Delphi had plagued me from kindergarten.

"I miss my parents and my best friend Raven...but other than that...I'm happy." I gave him a small smile.

He nodded, seeming relieved. "Good. I'll see you tonight." When he turned to walk away, I found myself wondering if Sawyer was happy. No one probably asked him that. I decided to do just that tonight on our date.

"Holy shit you look hot." Sage admired me from where she sat on my couch eating Oreos.

"Really? It's not too...revealing?"

Sage snorted. "Have you seen the other girls on their date nights?"

Yeah, I had. They fucking advertised it to everyone and made sure we all got a peek of what they were wearing: short dresses, cleavage, six-inch-high heels. I was modest, so this was a bit much for me. Sage had let me borrow a baby blue lace tube top that ended just below my breasts, and then I wore a high-waisted black silk skirt with a bow in the center. That all looked to preppy for me, so I threw on some black fishnets and my Doc Marten boots and I was ready to go. I showered in like four minutes, managing to shave and not cut myself, but there was no time to do my hair, so I let it air-dry in beachy waves.

The clock struck six p.m. and Sage jumped from the couch. "Okay, you *have* to kiss him tonight. I'm sure the other girls have and he needs to know you have chemistry."

I frowned. "Eww, you think he's been kissing all the other girls?"

She rolled her eyes. "No, not all of them, but I'm sure some are trying. Look, just be your amazing self and let him know you're interested, that's all."

Was I interested in a guy who might have potentially kissed forty-nine other girls?

Gross.

But my thoughts went back to what Sage had told me when she'd found him in Montana.

About wondering if anyone would ever love him back.

Walking over to the door, I threw it open to find Eugene and Walsh both dressed in suits. "Hey." I hadn't really seen Eugene much since that night with the vampire attack.

Walsh's gaze flicked behind me to Sage. He nodded once at her and then focused back on me.

Poor Sage.

"Good evening, Miss Calloway." Eugene gestured for me to walk with him and I did, letting the door close behind me. Sage would find her way back to her dorm eventually. Or not and she'd be there waiting to hear every word when I got back.

Either way, I wasn't worried about it.

One by one, the girls came out of the dorms to glare

me down as I passed. As we strode by Meredith and her evil clan, who were playing pool, they all stopped what they were doing and stared.

"Assassin," I heard one whisper loudly.

Oh God, are you serious? Nearly a month later and this assassin thing was sticking?

Great, just freaking great.

When we stepped outside the dorm, I paused, my breath catching in my throat. A long, sleek black limousine was waiting for me, with a driver opening the back door.

As far as I knew, Sawyer didn't send limos for the other girls...but maybe he did and I just didn't watch. I mean, I saw like five girls go out to dinner with him before it made me sick and I stopped watching. He could have...

Before I could overanalyze it, I stepped inside and expected Eugene and Walsh to follow me in, but they didn't. I was so used to having a shadow now, being without them was weird.

"Wow," Sawyer said from deep inside the limo and I jumped a little. "You look..." He paused, seemingly at a loss for words. In the dark car, all I could see were two amber eyes staring at me from the black depths.

"Beautiful?" I offered nervously.

The shadows moved as he crawled along the bench seat, making his way over to me slowly. When he reached me, the seat dipped with his weight as I leaned into him and he met my gaze. "Ravishing."

Heat flared to life inside of me, like an inferno that could only be cooled by one thing. I swallowed hard.

"I mean...you look okay," I joked.

He grinned, a soft chuckle emanating from his throat. "God, I love your sense of humor."

Shit, I didn't do real emotions, I mean I could, but I sucked at it. Being sarcastic was an easier shield for me to hide behind, but being with Sawyer felt so deep, like an endless ocean.

"It makes up for my terrible looks," I joked. I couldn't stop, they just kept fumbling out of me.

Before he could respond, the car stopped.

"That was short," I mused.

The door opened and Eugene helped me step out. What the...? Did he ride up front? Man, these guys were good at being seen when they wanted to be and scarce when needed. I took the guard's offered hand and stepped out onto...

A boat dock.

"Why are we—?" I started when a woman's shrill voice cut me off.

"Sawyer!" she screamed in excitement.

There were tons of people here. A red carpet had been set up and dozens of black limousines were waiting to drop more people off. I scanned the end of the red carpet and my eyebrows hit my hairline.

There was a cruise ship, or a yacht, or whatever the fuck rich people called those giant boats. It was docked and had the most beautiful white twinkling Christmas lights wrapped around the railing.

"Good evening, Mrs. Pepper." Sawyer nodded to the woman approaching us, but I could hear a hint of annoyance in his tone.

Pepper. As in Meredith Pepper?

Sawyer slipped his hand into mine and interlaced our fingers together, like it was no big deal. The brown-haired woman with way too much makeup on noticed we were holding hands and lifted a brow.

"I trust you've already got the list of top twenty? I'm sure Meredith is on it, no?" the woman said with a conspiratorial wink.

Sawyer gave a nervous laugh. "Should we really discuss these things at my father's birthday party?" He winked back.

She gave a short burst of nervous laughter and patted his chest. "You're right. Have fun at the party, dear."

When she walked away, I looked up at Sawyer, who stared down at me behind those thick black eyelashes. "You brought me as a date to the alpha's birthday party?"

Sawyer grinned. "He's just my dad, but yeah I wanted you here with me tonight."

That was…really sweet. Oh Lord, help me, I was falling hard. There was no way out of this unscathed. Not now.

I smiled. "And to think I almost didn't change.

What if I'd worn that 'single but not interested' shirt?" I scolded him as we started to walk the ridiculous red carpet.

Sawyer grinned, showcasing that damn sexy dimple and chin butt. "It would have been talked about for years to come."

We followed the throngs of people while I processed the fact that not only was I going on a yacht to the alpha's birthday party, I was doing so wearing a tube top, and with the alpha's son as my date.

I paused mid-walk. "I feel like I should change." People were wearing legit ballgowns.

Sawyer looked down at me, eyes hooded and shook his head. "You're perfect."

My cheeks reddened as he squeezed my hand and we continued to walk hand in hand onto the boat.

A piano was playing somewhere in the distance as we stepped on board, the sound setting the stage for what I was sure was a classy and expensive evening.

A man wearing a black suit bowed to us. "Sir Hudson."

Sawyer gave the man a genuine smile. "Roland, I'd like you to meet Demi Calloway."

He gestured to me and I smiled at the older man.

He bowed his head. "Good evening, Miss Calloway."

"Roland is our family butler. I've known him since before I could walk." Sawyer smiled warmly at the man.

"Hi." I waved shyly. "I left my butler at home."

Roland's calm façade broke as he chuckled and my gaze went to Sawyer, unsure if my joke was well received. He was grinning ear to ear, chin butt and dimple on full display.

Whew.

"Demi has a healthy sense of humor," Sawyer told his butler with a wink.

Roland nodded. "You've never brought a girl home with one of those. It's a nice change."

Oh snap.

Sawyer chortled and then someone pulled his arm and we were moving into the crowd and away from Roland. It was his mother, pulling us through the throng of people with a bright smile on her face. Well, pulling Sawyer and Sawyer pulling me. Leaning into my ear, Sawyer whispered, "Did my butler just totally burn me?"

I grinned. "Yep. Looks like you have horrible taste in women. Until me of course."

He smirked. "Of course."

After we were pulled into an opening, I noticed a stage set up at the back of the boat. To the right of it was a live piano player, and in the center was a giant white cake with blue piping around the edges.

Mrs. Hudson was wearing a floor-length black ballgown, and now that we had the space to face each other she gave her son a big hug. I dropped his hand, feeling awkward about holding hands in front of his mom, and he wrapped his arms around her.

"Good evening, Mother."

When she pulled back, her gaze went to me and I prepared for the scowl or a salacious scan of my dress, but to my surprise she pulled me in for a hug next.

"Oh." I was caught off guard, my arms coming up behind her back as she squeezed me.

When she pulled back, she was beaming. "Your father will be so delighted to see you both."

Sawyer slipped his hand back into mine and my stomach did flip flops.

Okay...

Maybe it wasn't a big deal, him bringing me to his dad's birthday party...but it felt like a big deal to me. Meeting his parents like this, holding hands in front of all the big mucky mucks of Werewolf City, it was...a lot.

But it felt so right. Sawyer had a way of making me feel like I belonged here, with him. I found myself wondering if he acted this way with all the girls, but somehow I didn't think so.

The next thing I knew, Curt Hudson was standing before me. His size and stature gave Eugene a run for his money. Dressed in a sleek black suit, he was the spitting image of his son, just with a few gray hairs at his temple, and a thick dark beard.

I'd sort of met him in the hallway when the vampires first attacked but not really, not like this.

"Demi, it's so lovely to officially meet the woman my

son won't shut up about," the alpha said, and Sawyer coughed loudly, shaking his head at his father.

I grinned, but when the alpha extended his hand to me, I froze.

Did I shake it? Kiss it? Curtsy?

Fuck, those etiquette classes were boring. I nodded off in them half the time. Deciding to go for a shake, I took his hand in mine and gave him a good hard squeeze.

"It's nice to formally meet you, sir. Happy Birthday."

He smiled, appraising me as we shook hands. A low buzz worked its way between our palms until it became a deep vibration and I yanked my hand back, giving my palm a curious look. He did the same, eyebrows drawn together.

"The man. The myth. The legend. The alpha!" a deep voice yelled over the PA system. Everyone started to clap and cheer as a spotlight shone on Sawyer's dad. The thunderous applause reached a crescendo and then a loud horn cut into the night as the boat left the dock. I swayed a little and Sawyer reached out to catch me by the waist. The clapping died down as his father took the stage to hug whoever the announcer guy was, and the piano started up again.

"Dance with me?" Sawyer asked, his hands still on my hips, blue eyes boring into my soul.

I just nodded. "Full disclosure, I've been napping in etiquette class, so if you want to waltz or anything, I'll just step on your feet."

A halfcocked grin pulled at the corner of his mouth and he chuckled. "There's no one quite like you, is there, Demi?"

Slowly, he pressed my body into his, as one of his arms slid around my back, the other taking my hand.

My body ached with need as I found my breath coming out in shuddered gasps. Being this close to him, to an unmated male wolf that I was *very* attracted to…it made my wolf absolutely pine. A carnal need washed over me and my mouth went dry. His scent, the heat from his body, the tight muscles under his arms, it made me want him in a way I'd never wanted a man before.

"I'm sorry I had to pick you last again, but tonight is special for my family and I wanted you here with me."

Aaaand he was fucking perfect.

I looked up at him and my gaze dropped to his lips. "I'm surprised your family is so nice to me. Poor banished girl comes from outside Magic City to assassinate son. It's not a good look for me."

Tipping his head back, he full-on laughed; the rumble of his chest against mine made my heart swell. His laugh was deep and hearty and contagious. When he brought his head back down to me, I was smiling.

He grinned. "You heard that rumor? I was hoping you wouldn't."

I snorted. "Why? I'm a big girl, I can handle it."

His face grew somber and he leaned into my ear:

"Because..." his breath washed over my neck, "everything I do now is to protect you."

Whoa.

Somehow I felt there was more to that comment than just protecting me from the rumor.

This was literally the best date I'd ever been on and it had only just begun, but there was an elephant in the room, something we still needed to talk about. Reaching up on my tippy toes, I pressed my lips to his ear. "Do you know what I am?"

His arms flexed, palm pressing firmly into my back, a clear physical reaction to my question, but when I met his gaze he just shook his head and looked back out over the lake.

Lie. I could tell.

Great. He was *almost* perfect. I mean, if my potential future wife could catch bullets and heal her hands seconds later, I would probably be in denial too, but we couldn't ignore this forever.

Whatever hopes I had that he was going to share with me what he knew were dashed. From now on, I'd have to do some digging of my own to find out what knowledge there might be about split shifting or whatever it was I did when my wolf came out.

"Sawyer, dear!" his mother called across the boat, and we broke apart, my body yearning for the heat and closeness of his. "Come greet Prime Minister Locke."

We turned, and I wasn't expecting the seven-foot-tall

light fey who stood next to Sawyer's dad. Inhaling sharply through my nose, I recognized the woody scent that all fey carried, but this one had an undertone of some seriously powerful magic. Magic smelled like electricity to me, almost like burned wires, but only faintly. This dude smelled of woods on fire, a very powerful fey, which explained why he was the prime minister of Fey City. The fey had a war ages ago and broke into two factions, dark fey and light fey. He was one of the good ones, although all fey were terrifyingly powerful, and no one was one-hundred-percent good.

The man greeted Sawyer, touching his palm to his own forehead and closing his eyes, as was custom with their kind. The few fey I knew from Delphi were total asshats, but I'd learned enough from them not to get myself into hot water with this one.

Hopefully.

Sawyer returned the greeting and then extended his hand, which the prime minister shook.

Interesting. They both honored each other's custom.

Mental note taken.

"It's good to see you, sir. This is my date, Demi Calloway."

The fey's eyes were so pale they were almost white—almost. They were a milk green that wasn't really of this world. Mixed with his silver hair and cream suit, he looked wholly out of place. His ears were sharply pointed and there was a glistening sheen to his skin that made him look like he was wearing highlighter makeup all over. His gaze raked over my face, and for the slightest second his brows drew together before a bright smile pulled at his lips.

"Greetings, prime minister." I placed my palm to my forehead and closed my eyes as he did the same.

When he extended his hand to shake mine, my wolf surged to the surface.

'Don't,' a voice said. My own voice, her voice, the voice of my wolf?

What the fuck?

Reaching out, I took his hand and a shock wave of electricity bolted up my arm. I hissed, trying to yank my arm back, when his palm clamped down on mine like a vise. Yanking, he pulled me closer and I stumbled forward into him.

"Hey!" Sawyer shouted as I crashed into the fey's chest. His nose went into my hair and he inhaled deeply, moaning the slightest bit in my ear like a horny old man.

Before I could process what was happening, I was yanked backward against Sawyer's chest.

"What the fuck was that!" Sawyer yelled, and some people nearby paused, their champagne flutes midair.

The alpha stared at the prime minister accusingly, while the fey's eyes pulsed from minty white to black.

"I'm feeling unwell suddenly. Mind if I lie down?" Locke asked, his voice a guttural sound that made my skin crawl.

"Certainly," Mrs. Hudson said, ever the good hostess, as she escorted him around the crowd and into the lower deck with worried glances back my way.

When he was out of earshot, Sawyer's father clicked his tongue. "I'm sorry about that, Demi. Prime Minister Locke is known for his obsession with young beautiful women, but that was not appropriate. Are you okay?"

I didn't realize my hands were shaking until I looked down at them. I was still smooshed with my back against Sawyer's chest, my breath coming out in ragged gasps.

Being held against my will was a *huge* trigger for me. I just needed a moment to get my bearings.

I nodded. "Just shook me up. If you'll excuse me." I pulled out of Sawyer's grasp and gave his father a weak smile before walking away from the noise and lights and crowd. Being yanked into an old man and *smelled* was my worst fucking nightmare. I'd frozen in the moment. All of my self-defense training left me and I just...froze. Now that I was able to process it, I was pissed. How fucking dare he! Why would he do that? In public, at the party of a diplomat? According to my mother, the fey, wolves, and witches had a very thin peace treaty. The slightest thing could shake it up and throw us all into the dark ages again. My mother said the balance between the races was an ever-present dance. The vampires, trolls and dark fey formed an alliance shortly after, and the only thing that held it together was that if one broke away and went to the other side, it would be uneven and start a war that one side would most definitely win.

I held the railing as the cold wind whipped across my face.

Maybe I overreacted...I mean, Sawyer's dad had said that fey were known for being sleazy with women. Maybe it was his custom...

But what about the buzzing through our hands? What was that?

"Did he hurt you?" a barely human growl called from behind me. I spun around, and upon seeing Sawyer with yellow eyes and pelts of dark gray fur rolling down his neck, I gulped.

I shook my head. "Just spooked me."

His brow furrowed, eyes going molten lava, absent of any blue. His wolf was fully in charge now.

"What did he whisper to you?" His voice was so freaky, I'd never heard anything like it before. It was like talking to a bear, if that were possible.

I shook my head. "Nothing...just smelled me and moaned."

Sawyer's canines descended, pressing onto his bottom lip. "That mother*fucker*, I'll kill him."

Oh shit.

Reaching out, I grasped the lapels of his jacket. "It's all good, I'm totally fine."

The boat suddenly stopped with a slight jerk and I frowned.

Sawyer held out his hand to me, which had lengthened to claws. "We're leaving. Eugene is lowering the row boat."

My eyes widened. "No. Oh my God, Sawyer, I'm fine. We don't—"

"*I'm* not fine." His jaw was so tight I thought he might break his teeth. "If we stay, my wolf will shift and rip out the prime minister's throat."

Holy fucking shit.

"Okay…I mean, when you put it that way. We should probably go." He took a shuddering breath as I grasped his hand, and then we were moving to the back of the boat.

"But your dad's birthday—"

"He understands," Sawyer growled.

Before I knew it, Sawyer and I had crawled down a ladder and into a rowboat with Eugene at the helm.

"Get us the hell out of here," Sawyer snarled.

Eugene looked at me, perplexed, but nodded.

When we were about fifty yards away, the yacht started up again and sailed away as the sun set on the horizon.

Sawyer held my hand so tightly it almost hurt, but I didn't think he realized it. It was like he was afraid of letting me go, and it touched my heart that seeing another man mistreat me wound him up so badly.

"Sawyer?" I called to him, and he looked over at me, eyes still orange. "I'm okay." I placed a hand on his chest and his eyes flickered blue. "I'm okay," I repeated again.

His breath shuddered, and then he leaned forward, touching his forehead to mine. His eyes slowly faded from orange to blue. "Demi, I will never let anyone hurt you. Ever."

My throat went dry. I believed him.

Could you fall in love with someone who you hadn't even kissed? Because I was falling for Sawyer Hudson, *hard*.

But was he falling for me? Or did I have too much baggage already?

By the time our limo stopped in front of my dorm, Sawyer was fully human again, but had stayed quiet throughout the entire drive. I was so used to the silence that I startled when he spoke. "Have you had any trouble keeping your wolf down?"

Okay, so were we finally going to go there...talk about my little split shifter problem?

I chuckled. "I was forced to keep my wolf down for over twenty years. What's another little while?"

He frowned. "Full moon is tomorrow night. The entire school goes for a pack run."

Oh...so that's why he was bringing it up.

Great.

I shrugged. "I'll say I'm sick."

He chewed his lip. "You've never been on a pack run during full moon. The collective magic that we use to shift is so strong...you won't be able to fight it."

"Oh...well..."

"I have an idea." He rubbed circles in the center of my palm. "You shift inside your dorm, early, and I'll come get you and walk your wolf over to the run site while your...other form stays in your dorm."

A grin broke out onto my face. "So I could run with you? With everyone?"

He nodded, looking hopeful. "Assuming there aren't any issues..."

I frowned. "Issues?"

He shrugged. "How far away can you be from your wolf? Does it hurt if you get too far? Things like that."

My eyes widened. "Oh...and if there are issues?"

He placed a possessive hand on my thigh. "Then I'll bring you right back to your dorm and say you are sick."

I nodded. It was worth a try, especially since I couldn't fake sickness and hide every month for the rest of the school year.

The door opened then and I saw a flash of Eugene before he was gone. Sawyer stepped out, pulling me up, but he didn't back away as I stood right up against his body. "I'm sorry tonight was a bust. I wanted you to have a really special date with me."

His warm body, pressed against mine, made me ache with need.

Please fucking kiss me.

"It was special." My breath was ragged as his hands came up to cup my face. I reached out and raked my fingers along his shirt, pressing into the hard muscles there, trying to communicate to him I wanted this.

Bad.

Mama needs some action.

He licked his lips and grinned, leaning forward.

"Sawyer!" a familiar female screamed right behind us, and his entire body tensed as he pulled away from me and faced Meredith.

"Oh, I'm sorry, I didn't know you were on a date," she said with a conspiratorial grin.

She looked pretty fucking pleased with herself for someone who didn't realize we were on a date.

"Well, I am." You could hear the annoyance in his voice.

"How was your dad's party? You know what, carry on, I'll just text you. See you tomorrow!" She waved us both off and then left.

For a split second I'd forgotten that I was competing for this man. I'd thought I was just over here falling in love with Prince Charming and ignored that he was dating forty-nine other fucking women.

"Night, Sawyer." There was a growl in my voice as I stepped away from him.

I thought he would let me go, like a sensible man, but instead he jumped out in front of me.

"Are you mad at me?" He looked sad.

I sighed. "I'm just not into this multiple women dating one guy thing. It's not for me. I also don't appreciate when I'm about to have a first kiss with a guy I like and his ex-girlfriend interrupts us."

He chewed on his bottom lip as if tempting me to give it another go. "You're right, she fucked that up and the mood is gone." Stepping closer to me, he leaned down and brushed his lips against my cheek. "I guess I'll just have to surprise you with the next one."

My eyelids fluttered closed as his breath washed over me.

Yes please.

I was about to tell him fuck it, the mood was back, when he pulled away and walked toward the limo, leaving me confused as all shit.

CHAPTER NINE

THE ENTIRE NEXT DAY I HAD ONE THING ON THE brain.

Sawyer.

I might as well have written our names inside of a heart on my notebook, because I had it bad. I kept replaying how upset he got that the prime minster had smelled me, and how he couldn't stand other men watching me dance, and how we'd finally almost kissed. Was I ridiculous for liking a guy that the entire female campus was dating?

Yes, yes I was.

The urge to pee overwhelmed me, so I stood and slipped out of my class. Navigating the halls, I stepped into the bathroom and went pee while thinking of Sawyer and his top twenty list. What came after that? Another month or round of dating and then top ten?

Did he date the final five girls for like six months? How was I going to handle that? Was he kissing other girls? Why the fuck did I have to fall for this guy? The one guy in the world who literally had to follow a set of rules in order to find his mate.

I needed to ask Sage about all this or dig back into the bylaws because I would probably go wild thinking of all of this stuff. I planned to head over to the library later and check out any books I could on split shifters or people who could separate from their wolf. Maybe while I was there, I would find a book on how to handle dating a guy who was also dating forty-nine other chicks.

Not likely.

After washing my hands, I slipped back out into the hallway, my mind swirling with a thousand things. I was so trapped in my thoughts, I barely noticed the blur of dark hair. Sawyer slipped out from an alcove and grasped the sides of my face. My heart hammered in my chest as he stroked my bottom lip with his thumb and gave me a cocky grin. Those piercing blue eyes stared into my soul as my breath came out in ragged gasps.

One of his hands dropped to my lower back and he tucked me into him, pulling me into the alcove and pinning my back against the wall.

Holy fuck. He was going to kiss me.

Leaning in, he passed my lips and went right for my ear, nibbling the flesh there and causing a moan to rip from my throat.

"I can't stop thinking about you," he whispered, dragging his lips along my jawline. My breath shuddered as his lips stroked up my cheek. "The way you smell, the way you walk." He pulled back and looked at me with blazing blue eyes. "The way you might taste."

I couldn't take it anymore, I was like a snake coiled and ready to strike. I yanked him forward and our lips crashed together in a hungry kiss. Warm soft lips melded with mine and an inferno exploded in my chest, traveling down my body. My lips opened as his tongue slipped inside and stroked mine, deepening the kiss. He growled, sexy and low, and I inhaled his breath as I clung to his neck, trying to press us closer together. His fingers slipped up the side of my neck as he tilted my head backward and took my bottom lip into his mouth, sucking.

Holy hell.

I'd never been this attracted to a guy, ever. If he pulled me in the janitor closet and asked me to go all the way, I would. He was like a drug and I couldn't get enough. It all felt so right, so good. His lips were on mine again, giving me slow but powerful kisses, and that's when the buzzing started—small vibrations at first, until it started to become more noticeable—my lips buzzing, and then my whole body, like I was made of electricity.

Sawyer moaned and then a white light sparked between us and he jumped backward, staring at me with wide eyes.

"What was that?" I asked, slightly scared but more turned on so my brain wasn't thinking properly.

His eyes darkened as his brows drew together in a frown. "I knew it," he muttered.

What? That made no sense to me. "Sawyer, what's going on? What was that?"

The vibrations reminded me of when I'd shaken his dad's hand, and also the prime minister's, but the light was new.

The air smelled of hot wires…magic.

Sawyer sighed, looking off down the hallway, where I was sure Eugene and Sage and whatever other guards stood waiting for us to finish our make out session. Finally, he met my eyes and his held such sadness; I wasn't prepared for it. "I'm going to have to do something you don't like, and you're going to need to trust me."

My eyes widened, but before I could ask him anything, he was gone, leaving me with swollen lips and a pounding heart.

Sawyer Hudson would be the death of me, that I was sure of.

I skipped lunch in the big dining hall and went right to the library with Walsh and Sage hot on my tail. They ate sandwiches and talked while I moved up to the counter to talk to the librarian. Sage said when she was on "shift" she needed to be all professional and couldn't sit with me or act all buddy-buddy, so I was on my own.

The freaking vibrating white light kiss with Sawyer had occupied my every thought, and I was determined to find out what it was. What *I* was.

Miss Lynch strode over to me once she saw me at the counter. "Can I help you, hun?"

I nodded, trying to figure out the best way to go about this. "So…I didn't exactly grow up in Wolf City, but my mom told me this story and I was wondering if you had any books about it?"

Her brows drew together. "What's the story called?"

Shit.

"I can't remember…but it was about a…split shifter who could walk around in human form for a while and her wolf stayed beside her."

Dawning shone on her face. "Yes. *The Cursed One.* I'm afraid that all the books on that creature have already been checked out."

Cursed one.

Creature.

My heart knocked so loudly against the walls of my chest, I could barely hear her.

"Who checked them out?" I knew the answer even before she told me.

"Sawyer Hudson. He's got them for…" She checked her tablet, swiping across the screen, "Oh. They've been removed from the library permanently." Her brows drew together in concern while the room spun around me.

Was I *cursed*? Was I a *fucking* creature?

Why would Sawyer hide this from me? Did he know or was he just checking out the books to find out?

Holy shifter.

The adrenaline was coursing so fast through my veins that my wolf came to the surface.

"Miss Calloway?" The librarian waved a hand in front of my face as my teeth lengthened.

My wolf rattled against my skin until my whole body vibrated. Reaching my hands out, I hugged myself tightly, trying to keep her in. She sensed danger in my fearful reaction of what the librarian had said.

"Sorry, I don't feel well," I told her.

She nodded knowingly. "Full moon. Happens to all of us, dear." I gave her a weak smile and turned around and ran. I ran past Sage and past Walsh, through two students trying to enter the library, and out into the garden. Students were lazing about, some of them in wolf form but most human.

'Stop it,' I told my wolf, as pelts of white fur ran down my arms.

Fuck, fuck, fuck.

The fact that my teeth could lengthen, I could howl and fur could grow on my arms, had to mean I was capable of a normal shift, of my human form shifting into a wolf...right?

As my shirt ripped, I realized I was out of time.

"Demi!" Sage called out from behind me as I took off into the woods. People turned to stare and I heard another seam of my shirt rip.

"Stop it!" I shouted out loud this time as I cleared the tree line. My eyes looked up to see that the moon was already out, faintly in the sky in the middle of the day. It had never affected me this badly, but then again, I'd had magical cuffs on and never lived in a pack before. Now that I was in the privacy of the thick trees, I let go of holding her in; it hurt too much, so I just took a deep breath and let go.

I expected to shift; I was a quarter of the way there with furry arms, lengthened teeth, and a bulked-out chest, but then my wolf began to separate from my body, the fur pulling off of me as my wolf went transparent, like a ghost so that she wouldn't tear my clothes, and then once she was out, she fully materialized.

What. The. Fuck?

How?

Why?

No!

"Demi!" Sage burst through the trees just as I slipped behind a giant boulder, crouching so that she and Walsh wouldn't see me.

When she skipped to a stop before my wolf, I blinked and suddenly I was looking up at her from the view of my wolf.

Sage sighed in relief at the sight of my wolf. "You fucking scared me! I thought something was wrong. First full moon?"

My wolf nodded up and down and she grinned. Walsh burst into the bushes, gun drawn, and my wolf growled for a slight second until she realized who it was.

She trusted Walsh, and Sage too.

"It's her first full moon. I'm gonna shift so we can run," she told Walsh, and started to pull her top off.

His gaze flicked to her black bra for a millisecond before he nodded once and gave us his back. It was so weird to be in my human form hiding behind a rock but also feel myself as a wolf, looking at Sage as rust-colored pelts of fur broke out on her skin. I could see from both realities, and it made me feel a little paranoid. What if this wasn't real and I was losing my mind?

Sage nipped at my tail, pulling me from my dark thoughts, and took off into the forest as my wolf bounded after her. The wind rushed through my fur as I jumped over damp earth and a fallen log. My paws pounded the mossy floor and tears lined my wolf's eyes.

The feeling…it was…

'I'm free,' I thought. *'I'm finally free.'*

This was what my wolf had wanted all along. Every time one of those assholes at Delphi riled me up and poked my wolf, daring her to come out, this is what she wanted, to run free, no more cuffs, no more suppression; she could protect me when needed unlike that night with the vampires. It was weird to live with the guilt that you weren't able to protect your own self during an attack. The night of my rape, I'd been so helpless without my wolf. Pinned down, beaten into submission, my wolf tried, but with the cuffs, I was just human. No match for one vampire, never mind four.

This feeling, her being out and running with Sage like a real wolf…it was everything.

"I can hear your heartbeat, you know?" Walsh turned and faced the boulder I was hiding behind.

Fuck.

I froze, not even daring to breathe.

"Sawyer is my best friend. He told me about…your condition, so that I could better protect you."

I slowly stood, and tentatively caught his gaze.

He took one look at me and shook his head. "I'm going to have to tell Sawyer what happened today."

Unfortunately, I was not wearing my *Snitches Get Stitches* shirt, but I really wanted to say it.

"Come on? What am I, twelve? You gonna tell Daddy on me?" I crossed my arms and pinned him with a glare. I didn't want Sawyer knowing I almost shifted in the library, not after our weird yet amazing kiss.

A slow grin pulled at his lips and I realized that he was pretty good looking when he wasn't scowling. "I'm going to have to tell Sawyer you called him daddy too. He'll like that."

My eyes bugged. "Don't you dare."

He shrugged. "I have orders. Come on, let's get you back to your dorm and I'll have Sage bring your wolf there."

"She doesn't know?" I asked.

He shook his head. "Just me, Eugene, and Sawyer."

Great.

Following him out of the tree line, I scanned the area with paranoia.

They know, they all know that I'm human and my wolf is out there with Sage...

Except no one spared us more than half a glance.

This is so weird.

I was walking with Walsh, but at the same time fully aware of chasing Sage to a creek and rolling around in the grassy moss. How far apart could we get? Hopefully far enough...

Walsh silently led me back to my dorm. When Meredith tried to engage in conversation with him as we passed the common area where she sat with her preppy friends, he ignored her. Making it back to my dorm, I slipped inside while Walsh stood outside my door like a sentinel.

I sat on my bed, nervously drumming my fingers along the satin sheets. Being without my wolf felt... weird. I felt half empty, and I was due in my next class in like fifteen minutes.

'Come back to my dorm. We need to get to class.' I tried talking to myself which only increased the feeling that I was ridiculous.

'Coming,' a voice huskier than mine, but still mine, answered back.

Holy shit. I ran my hands through my hair, trying not to think too much about it. Was I two people? How? Chewing off all my nails over the next three minutes, I jumped up a little when I heard Sage's voice.

"She's good I think, she's just too shy to shift outside. I couldn't find her clothes," Sage said just outside the door.

"I got them. Torn to bits." Walsh cleared his throat loudly and I slipped back into my bedroom, tossing off my clothes to find new ones. This was going to be a hard lie to keep. I knew he had opened the door and let my wolf in. I could see through my wolf, which I would never get used to. Then he closed the door as she padded down the hall and into the closet where I was. When I saw her, tongue lolled out of her mouth, tail wagging like a happy dog, tears sprang in my eyes.

"You liked that, huh?" I knelt down and she came to me, nuzzling my hand.

'We need it. To be free,' she told me, and I nodded. We did.

"Well, Sawyer is coming to get us tonight to do it again with the whole pack." I rubbed her behind the ear and she gave me a wolfish grin. I'd finished dressing and now stood.

"Come on, we gotta get to class." I tapped my chest.

Jumping up onto her hind legs, she put her paws on

my chest and went ghostly transparent as she melted into me. A slight painful zapping sensation crawled along my skin, but only for a second. It was getting less painful, but still weird as all hell.

"Demi? Ready?" Sage's singsong voice called into the apartment.

I peeked out of my room and gave her a shy smile. "Ready."

She grinned when she saw me. "Your wolf is fast. You're going to give the boys a run for their money tonight."

I frowned. "What do you mean?"

We stepped out into the hallway and she leaned into me. "Sawyer, Walsh, and Quan hold the record for fastest run in wolf form. It's kind of an untold thing that every full moon run is actually a race."

A race?

Okay, no pressure.

"Well, I don't want to race anyone." I laughed nervously.

"You should. Some of these boys need their egos knocked down a little. Including my cousin."

I grinned. "All right, see you tonight, then."

She nodded and stepped back into line with Walsh behind me, back on guard duty.

Now that I'd shifted, I was feeling confident that Sawyer's plan tonight would totally work. I would stay in my apartment while he took my wolf on a run with the pack. Maybe this freak creature that I was didn't need to be a bad thing. Maybe I could have the best of both worlds...

CHAPTER TEN

LATER THAT NIGHT, WHEN SAWYER KNOCKED ON THE door a little earlier than planned, I was nervous but ready. I'd just been adjusting the aperture setting on my camera to practice shooting products.

Opening the door, I grinned at him. "Hey."

His face was stock still, no emotion. "Hey." He was hiding something behind his back.

Flowers? No. Not with that face.

"Everything okay?" I hedged, my eyes going to Walsh in the hallway.

You rat! Probably told him I almost shifted in public today.

"Can I come in?" he asked.

I stepped aside, letting him fully into the apartment.

"Look, I know today wasn't ideal but—"

"But you almost showed everyone what you are," he growled as I shut the door behind him.

I frowned, suddenly getting pissed. "What am I, Sawyer? Because I can't seem to figure it out seeing as though all of the books are missing from the library and you won't tell me what the fuck is going on!"

He sighed, pulling a torn book page from behind his back and handing it to me. "I remember reading it when I was twelve. It scared the shit out of me. Gave me nightmares for weeks."

I grabbed the torn paper with a shaky hand, stroking the image stamped on the upper half of the page. It was a girl on her knees, screaming up at the moon while a wolf crawled out of her chest.

"I think this is what you are," Sawyer said, and reached up to stroke my cheek. "If anyone were to find out about this...about you..."

I grasped the page and started to read.

The Cursed One is a creature born of the werewolf race, who goes through a trauma so severe it causes a soul splice.

The soul splice is a process that happens to a werewolf creature when they go through a disturbance so horrifying in human form, that their wolf splits from their soul, standing outside the human's body so that they don't have to experience or remember it.

Tears streamed down my cheeks as I swallowed a sob and kept reading. My rape. My soul split so that I didn't have to experience the full extent of that night.

In doing so, this creates a magical vacuum, sucking

into itself all kinds of magic from the ethers. When the wolf re-enters the human, they are never fully fused, now able to split shift, stay human and wolf, walking side by side. But eventually the magic the creature has taken in starts to express itself. Mental compulsion, telekinesis, strength and speed ten times that of a vampire—

My eyes darted to the final line. The word *death* pulling at my attention.

These creatures are like a powerful drug to all six types of the magical races. If their essence is fed upon, they give the feeder extreme strength, speed, and all of the powers they possess. It has been determined that they are too strong and dangerous to be allowed to live. They would be hunted their whole life, which is an inhumane way to exist, and no one should have that much power. It is recommended by the Magical Creature Council that they be put to death, and is referenced in werewolf bylaw 390.01: Any Split Shifter Cursed Ones discovered will be put to death.

I dropped the page and it fluttered to the ground like a delicate feather and not the dangerous and heavy thing that it was. My hands shook as tears lined my eyes.

Sawyer stepped closer to me, still one arm behind his back, and held me as I sobbed into his chest.

"Demi..."

I pulled back and looked up at him, his expression

painful. "Did...something traumatic happen to you when you were younger? Something like the book says?"

He was trying to figure out if I met all the requirements of this cursed creature.

I just nodded, and his shoulders sank.

My mind was playing catch up. "Our kiss. The vibrating...the light."

He gulped, his Adam's apple bobbing. "I think the vibrating was your essence. I think I accidently..." He released a shaky breath. "Fed on you."

"The prime minister..." My voice trailed off and he nodded.

The fey must have sensed what I was and tried to...

I shivered thinking about it.

"I'm never going to let anything bad happen to you. Do you understand me?" His voice was a low growl and I nodded.

I believed him. By some trick of fate, this dude liked me and wanted to protect me.

"The light?" I asked him, so completely lost.

A slight smile pulled at his lips as he stroked my cheek. "That was something else."

There was a knock at the door, pulling us from this moment. "Everyone is ready to run! Meet us outside," Sage shouted and then retreating footsteps could be heard down the hall.

His lips turned into a frown. "Remember when I said

I was going to have to do something you didn't like? But that I needed you to trust me?"

My brows drew together as I looked up at him and nodded.

"I'm sorry," he whispered as the bite of steel came around my left wrist.

No.

Before I knew what was happening, he reached out and slammed a cuff on my right. Searing green magic flared up my arms as I fell to my knees, gasping.

He...*he caged me*. Imprisoned me all over again, I couldn't believe it. My wolf rattled against me, shaking my chest as pelts of fur rippled down my arms, but it was no use. She was trapped. There was no electric shock so these cuffs must be different, but it didn't matter, they were still cuffs.

A sob caught in my throat as I looked up at a tortured-looking Sawyer. He looked on the verge of tears, holding the sides of his face like he couldn't believe he'd just done this.

He fell to his knees before me, looking absolutely distraught. "I'm trying to keep you alive, if my father, or—"

"Fuck you!" I screamed, a half sob and half howl. Tears rolled down my face as the realization that I would be trapped as a human forever tore into me. But it wasn't just that...it was that the man I'd been falling for had done this to me, *without asking*. Would I have let him if he had asked? No. My wolf wouldn't have allowed it, but to not be given a choice...

"Demi." His voice broke. "I like you so fucking much, I just—"

"Get out!" I roared, reaching out to plant my palms on his chest and shoving him backward. He landed on his butt and I sprang up to my feet, running into my bedroom and slamming the door behind me. What was the point of me even coming here? What was the point of him "freeing" me only to be bound once again?

It's like I was back at Delphi, back inside a cage where I couldn't be myself.

He knocked on the bedroom door a few times but I barely heard him through my sobbing into the pillow.

CHAPTER ELEVEN

THE NEXT TWO WEEKS DRAGGED ON PAINFULLY slow. Everyone and their fucking mother had heard about Sawyer cuffing me. Rumors swirled about me not being able to control my wolf, or about me attacking someone and that's why he had to cuff me. But the best rumor was that he had in fact found out that I was an assassin, and I wore these cuffs to keep from killing him.

Fuck my life.

Sage was so confused, kept asking me why Sawyer would do that and pried for more information, but I was too depressed to tell her everything. If this was my life now, caged inside my body, I'd better get used to it and there was no sense in telling her now.

Sawyer had sent approximately one giant bouquet of flowers per day since he cuffed me, and it was getting to the point where I couldn't walk around my apartment.

He'd even been commenting all these cute apologetic things on my Instagram photos. Sage was ignoring her cousin in solidarity on my behalf, and I was turning down date requests from him daily. Let him go out with the other nineteen girls; I couldn't be with a man who wanted to see me imprisoned, even if it was because he thought he was protecting me. This was no way to live, especially after getting my taste of freedom.

Yesterday I'd found out that I made the top twenty.

Yay. Cue sarcasm.

"I've got a surprise for you tonight." Sage turned to me as I pushed my eggs around my plate. Sawyer was eating breakfast with Meredith and Priya, while not so casually sneaking glances back at me. Today I was wearing a custom t-shirt Raven had made me that said *Feeling Stabby* with a little wolf cartoon holding a knife.

It perfectly displayed my mood. Raven and my parents sent weekly care packages with human candy I didn't get in Werewolf City, and we talked often, but I was starting to feel lonely and homesick.

"I hate surprises," I informed her as I watched Sawyer take a drink of his orange juice. Even his jawline was attractive.

Asshole.

Sage waved her hand in front of me. "Hello."

My gaze snapped to hers. "What?"

"You're going to like this surprise. Trust me." She grinned. She was such a good friend, doing her best to take my mind off of the fact that I was a prisoner in my own body.

Giving her a weak smile, I stood. "Okay. Thanks. I gotta run. See you later."

She frowned. "Yeah...later, Demi."

When I got to class, I immediately threw myself into my art. Taking pictures was the only thing keeping me sane right now. I'd talked Sage into letting me do a series of four shots of her a few weeks ago and they all turned out amazing. Her vibrant red hair against the muted background I'd chosen was perfect.

"These are impressive, Miss Calloway," Professor Woods spoke from behind me as I laid the prints out on my desk.

"Thanks. I was thinking of doing a nature series next."

He nodded. "Well, you might just get your wish, because today we are all going on a field trip with Professor Hines' class after lunch."

Excitement thrummed through me. "Where are we going?"

Please say something cool like to snap pictures of a cemetery or something.

"The Dark Forest." He winked and moved on to the next student.

It sounded ominous, but I had no idea what the Dark Forest was.

"Holy shit," Chris whisper-screamed from behind me. "The Dark Forest? I wonder how the alpha approved that?"

I spun, stepping over to his and James' shared table as I fiddled with my wide-angle lens. "What do you mean? Is it haunted or something?" I whispered back.

Chris chuckled. "Yeah, by wolf rebels and hybrids that want to cut our throats out."

I froze, looking up at him. "What?"

Chris and James shared a look that said "Aww, the cute blond is an idiot," before leaning back into me. "Seriously? Your parents didn't tell you about the Paladin family? Or the Ithaki?"

The whati? Hadn't Sage mentioned the Paladins at the welcome dinner?

I shook my head. "Who are the Paladins?" Sounded like some made up fantasy stuff to me.

Chris chortled. "The original alpha royals. Before the Hudson family *stole* the crown."

James slapped him on the chest. "That's not true, they weren't *royal*, just badass. Back when you became alpha by fighting, and not by bloodline."

My eyes bugged. "And they are still alive?"

James nodded. "They live in the woods like animals. I heard they don't even have plumbing or toilets. They attack us every once in a while, but obviously our army is stronger."

Holy crap. Between the vampires and these... Paladin's, Wolf City was way more dangerous than I thought.

"And the other group? The Itakie?"

Chris laughed. "*Ithaki*. They're worse than the Paladins, they—"

"Okay, class!"

Before I could respond, Professor Woods called our attention to the front and I pushed what James had said to the back of my mind.

"Please finish up any work you have in the darkroom today and post your final pieces in the display cases out in the hall. The staff will be voting on who should be showcased in the end-of-year exhibit."

We scurried to get our work together, James running into the darkroom and Chris mounting his photos to the blackboard. I snatched up my prints of Sage and slipped out into the hall to tack them up into the cases. I decided to keep them raw with no border or anything fancy, let Sage be the beautiful part of the piece.

Reaching the first case, I flipped the lock and opened it up, pulling some of the pins out and sticking them on the corners of the photo. I was halfway through my second photo when I smelled him.

My heart hammered in my chest as I ignored the footfalls and earthy scent of sexy almost-alpha male. I'd singlehandedly avoided being alone with him for two weeks, but I guess my time was up.

"Demi?" His voice held mock shock, "Weird seeing you here. We've got to stop meeting like this."

I positioned a pin between my fingers and spun, pointing it at him threateningly. "You're premed. You have no classes in this building, which means you're stalking me."

His face fell and he sighed deeply as he stared at the cuffs on my wrists. "Demi, you've been ignoring me..."

I scoffed. "Sawyer, you *imprisoned* me!" I held up a cuffed arm and shook it in front of his face.

He stepped closer to me and I held the pin up, narrowing my gaze at him.

He produced his arm, shoving it right in front of my face. "Go ahead. Stab me if it will make you feel better."

I snort-laughed, I couldn't help it. He was funny and fucking adorable. "Eugene will kill me." I gestured to the giant man standing thirty paces back who was trying to pretend he wasn't looking at us.

Sawyer shook his head. "No. I deserve it. Quick, before I change my mind." He mock flinched as if anticipating great pain.

Part of me really wanted to drive this pin into his fucking arm for what he did to me and my wolf.

So I did.

Without thinking, I rammed the pin into his arm, only stopping when he hissed. We both yanked back at the same time.

"Holy shit! You really stabbed me." He looked at me with half wonder, half amusement.

I snorted, falling into peals of laughter, and looked at the end of the pin. "This has your blood on it. I could take it to a witch and make a nice voodoo doll to cause you even more pain."

A seriousness clouded his face. "Oh, Demi, nothing would cause me more pain than knowing I hurt you and your wolf."

My gaze went to the red pinprick dot of blood on his arm which had already crusted over and healed. He reached out, slowly, giving me time to back away, and grasped the bottom of my chin, forcing me to look into his eyes. "Will you let me explain? Meet me for dinner tonight?" He ran his thumb over my bottom lip and I swallowed hard.

I knew what he was going to say, that he was trying to protect me. I'd read the book page. It said that I should be put to death; they even put it in the bylaws. But to have him force the cuffs on me, against my will, it was like being raped all over again.

"There's more you need to know..." He looked over his shoulder to make sure we were still alone. "I've got one shot at picking the perfect mate and I don't want to fuck that up with you."

The air charged with electricity.

Wait, what? What did that mean? That he thought *I* might be the perfect mate?

My head spun with his words as he leaned in and whispered into my ear. "Meet me tonight? My dorm? I'll cook for you. Don't make me beg. I will if I have to."

There was something so incredibly sexy about a dominant future alpha saying they would beg for you. With a shaky breath, I nodded and he started to pull away, which made me realize I didn't want him to go. His smell, his heat, his everything. I needed it.

I wrapped my fingers behind his neck, crushing my lips to his. A moan let loose from his throat as I slipped my tongue into his mouth and stroked against his own. Reaching out with my teeth, I nipped his bottom lip harder than I normally would and then pulled back to meet his searing blue eyes. "If you *ever* force something on me again without talking to me first..." I shoved one of my cuffs in his face to indicate what I meant. "I'm done."

His brow furrowed. "If it means I've saved your life, then it's a risk I'm willing to take."

Now it was my turn to furrow my brow. Did he *really* think someone would kill me because of what I was? His dad, his sweet dad who I'd met and seemed as alpha as a stuffed teddy bear, would kill me over some bylaw? But the blazing yellow protective eyes that stared back at me said yes, he did believe that, and maybe I should too.

Fuck.

I released him and he plucked the pin out of my fingers. "I'll be confiscating this, Miss Calloway. No voodoo dolls for you. I'll see you tonight. After Sage's surprise."

I grinned and watched him walk away, more confused than ever before. How did he know about Sage's surprise? I thought they weren't talking.

Maybe Sawyer knew more than he let on and maybe he *had* saved my life. Maybe binding my wolf had stopped the scent or whatever was leading the vampires to me. Shit, I didn't know what to think anymore. But I couldn't wait until dinnertime to find out.

The drive to the Dark Forest took about half an hour. It was beautiful to weave through the mountains, houses topped high on the hills, verdant green trees dotting the landscape. When we reached a small access road, the school bus took a hard left and I clutched my seat to keep from tipping into Walsh.

"Now, the waterfall assignment is broad. I don't want to stifle anyone's creativity, so if you want to hike to the top and take a picture looking down in a bird's eye view or whatever, it's fine with us." Professor Woods looked at Professor Hines, who shared a conspiratorial wink. They would make a cute couple. Lord knows they were always batting eyes at each other.

"Just stay on *our* side of the woods." Professor Hines tone dropped into ominous levels and I perked up.

"Werewolf City's border is marked with red stakes every few feet. Do not step over into the Wild Lands."

Walsh shifted uncomfortably next to me and I frowned. "What is the Wild Lands?" I whispered to him.

"Look..." He ignored my question and I peered up to see the bus drive out from the thick canopy. As the treed road opened up into a green valley, the breath hitched in my throat.

"Holy crap," I breathed.

Two giant mountains stood next to each other like old friends. Between them was a bright green valley full of lush green growth and mossy sponge covering the ground. The mountain to the right, the slightly bigger one, had a cobalt blue vein of water pouring down its middle. It was like we were at Yellowstone National Park or some other famous place, but instead we were in an unknown portion of Werewolf City, gazing at the most beautiful waterfall I'd ever seen.

Walsh pointed to a small cluster of wood cabins to the right. "I used to come here as a kid. My mom has a cabin over there." I'd never spoken to him this much, but seeing his home seemed to bring the chattiness out of him.

On the other side of where his mom's cabin was, there were a line of reddish-orange flags in the dirt, clearly demarcating a property line. I thought about what Professor Woods said about staying on "our side" and frowned.

I wished my parents had told me more about this place. I had little idea who the Paladins were, or about any of this stuff.

We parked the bus in a designated spot and disembarked, taking in the picturesque surroundings. The beautiful sound of over thirty students' shutters opening and shutting in tandem made a grin pull at the edges of my lips. I decided to try something different. Pulling a spare lens out of my bag, I held it up, looking through it about twelve inches away, and then snapped a picture of the lush landscape through the lens, through my camera, catching my fingers holding it in the frame as well.

"That's going to be a good one," Professor Woods murmured beside me.

I gave him a wry smile, so grateful for this field trip.

"Let's start hiking! We aren't even to the really pretty stuff yet," Professor Hines said.

I'd worn my white Converse knockoffs, which I had a feeling I was about to trash. Mental note to get hiking boots with Sawyer's money, because now that I had these cuffs on I felt less bad about spending his cash. If he was going to be a dick and cage me, I was going to retaliate with shopping therapy.

"Oh look!" Jennie pointed to a thick fern bush and I followed her gaze.

It took a second for my eyes to adjust, but when I realized what it was, I gasped a little.

Whoa.

There must be over a hundred orange and black butterflies dripping down the branches like a living sculpture.

I screwed on my macro lens and took an amazing zoomed-in picture of the texture of the wings.

Click, click, click. We all snapped pictures.

"The monarchs. We only get them for a few months and then they're back on their way to Mexico," Professor Hines said.

After that, we silently settled into the hike across the valley and over to the base of the waterfall.

"Can I go in the water?" Jennie asked.

I liked Jennie, she was chill, low maintenance, and didn't make the top twenty with Sawyer, so she wasn't an asshole to me like the other girls.

"Absolutely," Professor Woods said.

Chris pulled a camera drone from his backpack and I scowled at him. "Cheater."

He grinned. "I'm not climbing all the way up there for a good shot."

"I am!" I announced.

"Me too," a dude named Samson said, and started to hike in that direction.

"Wonderful! It seems you all have an idea of the shot you want to get. Take your time. We have three hours slotted for the field trip."

I started to hike up the well-worn path to the right of the waterfall, and Walsh stepped in behind me. "You don't have to go up with me," I told him.

He just grumbled under the hood of his jacket, which was now pulled up because the waterfall was spitting mist at us when the wind changed directions.

Okay, I guess my chatty Walsh was gone.

It was a steep hike. Like a freaking stair stepper. My thighs burned when we got halfway, and I stopped with Samson to pull water from my backpack and take a long swig. Walsh didn't look nearly as out of breath as Samson and I, and I wondered what kind of exercise regimen Sawyer's guards were on. Because clearly I needed it.

"Screw this. Good enough," Samson groaned, and walked over to the edge, starting to snap pictures.

I frowned. "Not going to the top?"

He shook his head. "Too much work for a photo."

I swallowed my scoff and nodded. Photography was my life. Most of the time it was taking a photo in a moment, but others it was waiting hours for a bird to show up and drink from the bowl of water you set out, or to hike a mountain and get that shot that's in your head. Photography was freezing your memories so other people could view them forever, and that's what I was determined to do today.

I took off up the mountain with fierce determination. I wasn't going to back down because something was hard—what kind of person did that? No one I could ever respect or be with. I glared at Chris' drone as it flew down from the top, already having taken its amazing photos and now done. An annoyed growl ripped from my throat and I picked up the pace even faster.

"You're pissed about something," Walsh commented, barely winded at my side.

I gave him a long side-look. "Yeah, it just seems like everyone in Werewolf City is used to having things handed to them on a silver platter."

A slow smirk pulled at his lips. "And you're not?"

"No," I growled, and pushed harder into the hike. It hit me then, I was so mad. Mad at Werewolf City, mad at Curt Hudson and his stupid bylaws, mad at the system. Why did my mother and father get kicked out? Why did I have to grow up without a pack, in a school of misfits who shit on me every day, when these Wolf City kids were being spoon-fed every drop of luxury. I guess I was glad it happened that way, it made me who I was. I wasn't the girl who took the easy shot.

Before I realized it, I'd reached the peak of the mountain. It was craggy and pointy, with a path only about twelve inches wide. If you slipped forward, you would fall down the front of the waterfall, and if you slipped backward you would fall down the back of the mountain.

Note to self: Don't do either.

I peered to my right, down the backside of the mountain, and noticed those little red boundary flags and a blur of motion as something moved in the thick tree line down there.

A Paladin?

My heart hammered in my chest as I stared at the spot, but I didn't see any more movement and started to think I was making it up. Picking up my camera, I took a picture of the boundary flags, reminding myself to ask Sage more about it. I stepped about five paces along the path until I was directly up to the waterfall, hovering right over it. Part of the mountain was flat, bringing water from a river somewhere, but the part I stood on, that I'd just climbed up, steeply cut off the back like it had been shorn off in an earthquake or something.

Nature was crazy.

Pulling my camera up to my eye, I stepped forward and looked down over the waterfall.

"Be careful," Walsh warned.

I pulled the camera back and looked at him, twenty feet away back at the path that led down the mountain. "Come here, you *gotta* see this. It's amazing."

He shook his head and crossed his arms over his chest. "I don't like heights."

I chuckled. "Okay."

Looking back down through my lens, I couldn't help but feel a thrill run through me at the sheer size of the height I was standing at. Water flowed unrestricted down the mountain, slower at first, until it crashed into a mass of white rapids and turbulence.

I hung my head directly forward and snapped the picture. And that's when I felt my balance go wonky.

The ground was wet, so when I went to take that half a step forward to get the shot, my foot gave way.

Oh hell no.

I felt myself fall forward, toward the waterfall a little, and panicked, throwing my weight backward to counter the move.

Bad idea.

"Demi!" Walsh screamed as I overshot the path and began to fall completely backward. My ass hit the ground hard and then I was sliding. Pain laced up my back as I slid like a kid on a snow day, except without a sled.

Oh fuck, was all I could think as I dropped my camera around my neck and started to grasp at ferns, tree trunks, anything to slow my fall.

That's when I started to roll. I hit a little rock shelf, went airborne, and when I came down on my left shoulder, something snapped. I wailed in pain and I just started rolling. Like a fucking bowling ball, I tumbled down the mountain, Walsh was screaming my name like a madman and I just kept thinking: *How is it not over yet? How am I still falling?* My wolf surged to the surface, but the cuffs kept her at bay as I rolled and rolled, until I felt sick and battered and half dead. Pain throbbed and sliced through my entire body as the mountain chewed me up and spit me out.

With a grand finale, my head smacked the side of a rock and everything went blurry.

I cried out as pain laced behind my skull, and I finally stopped rolling, skidding to a stop on the ground.

With a shaky hand, I used my right arm to grab the side of my hair, and upon feeling the sticky wetness there, I pulled it back with a whimper.

Walsh's voice felt far away and warbled. I was confused.

What happened? Where was I? How did I get here?

Shit, I hit my head.

Oh God, my shoulder.

I focused on Walsh's voice, something familiar, something that I knew would keep me safe as I lay there and felt sleepiness work its way into my body. A twig snapped, and then a giant of a man, big enough to rival Eugene, stepped over and crouched in front of me. A man about sixty years old stood shirtless with bright blue tribal war paint on his chest and face. A necklace made of tiny, sharpened bones hung around his neck. He bent down and looked at me, frowning.

I was scared of him for a moment. I mean who was this? A Paladin? Had I rolled onto "their" side?

Everything was confusing.

When he crouched down and looked at me, I was taken back with how kind his blue eyes were. Eyes that kind couldn't hurt me, right?

He reached out a hand to place two fingers at the pulse on my neck and I smelled him.

Wolf.

Dominant.

Magic?

Satisfied with my pulse, he picked up my right, good hand, and inspected the arm cuff, then he leaned down and smelled my wrist, looking back at me wide-eyed, his eyes the color of the waterfall.

"You need to be more careful, pup. I've seen the Ithaki drain your kind in less than a minute," he whispered, looking behind him as if he'd heard something.

Ithaki? Drain my blood? Maybe my head was still concussed, because I was confused about what he was saying. Walsh still sounded so far away, screaming for the guy to leave me alone. I just wanted to sleep. I groaned, my eyelids closing. The man lightly slapped my face, causing my eyelids to flutter open.

"No sleep," he told me, and looked back up to where Walsh was screaming.

I whimpered as the pain of everything that just happened seeped into my body all at once, and the adrenaline left me. "It hurts."

He frowned and then nodded. Reaching into a pouch at his waist, he pulled out a small white root. "Chew." He shoved it in my mouth and I nearly spat it out. It was bitter as all hell, but within a few bites I'd crushed the outside and a sweetness coated my tongue as some of the pain was chased away along with my foggy thoughts.

Oh God. I fell. I fell *really* bad. The last few minutes

were coming back to me now and how badly I'd royally screwed up.

"Get the fuck away from her!" Walsh screamed, closer now.

The man looked over at Walsh sadly and then down at me. "Stupid city wolves. Have you been with them this whole time?" he grumbled, and started to unfold an animal skin from his waist pouch.

Leaning down over me, he lay the animal skin blanket over me, and that's when I realized I was shivering. He picked up my cuff again and inspected it. "Won't heal with this on," he growled, as if he were angry.

What would a random forest caveman wolf have to be angry about on my behalf?

I pointed at him, finally feeling the effects of the pain-relieving root. "Paladin?"

His blue eyes flicked to mine and he nodded, just once, before his head was sliced from his body.

Terror ripped through me as I screamed bloody murder. Crimson blood splattered over me as the man's head fell to my side and his body tumbled forward.

Walsh was no longer human, because instead of hearing him scream my name, I now just heard the howl of a wolf.

Looking up at the shadow that crossed over my face, I saw a...I don't know what it was. A pointed-ear fey man that smelled of a wolf? He was dressed in the same crude homemade clothing style as the nice man who'd just tried to help me, but he looked much more sinister. Black hair hung to his waist in a thick braid, and he had small pockmark scars over his greasy face. With one kick, he knocked the head of the Paladin away from me and then leaned down to smell my neck. It was then that I saw a dozen more men behind him, all grinning and holding long, curved and serrated, sickle-type blades.

I screamed again, trying to move, but when I did pain just laced up my body in all directions and I felt dizzy.

Taking a deep inhale of my scent, he grinned. "Little demon, you're coming with me."

Then he struck the side of my temple with the blunt end of a sword and I was met with blackness.

CHAPTER TWELVE

When I came to there was a period of confusion. I smelled burning meat, and that bitter yet sweet taste was still in my mouth. Pain wasn't even a word I could use to describe how I felt. Torture was more apt.

Everything hurt.

My skin, my muscles, my eyeballs, maybe even my eyelashes, I wasn't sure if there was a part of my body that *didn't* hurt.

That's when everything came back to me in hazy flashes.

I fell.

Bad.

The Paladin man had tried to help me and…I choked on a sob as I remembered his head coming off like that.

Light flickered behind my eyelids and I realized I

hadn't opened them yet. Springing them open, I tuned into the voices in the room.

A man was standing over a woman who sat in the corner of the room. I was in some type of hut with bamboo slat floors and bamboo slat walls, crudely tied together with twine.

"The skin is too damaged from the accident, I will have to sell her in pieces," the woman was saying as bile crept up my throat.

The man growled. "Then we will heal her first and we can get a better price."

The woman was silent. "You're lucky the demon has been bound by the cuffs, or she'd have ripped you limb from limb."

The man snarled. "Can you heal her or not? I'll give you ten percent of what she fetches at market."

The woman sighed. "Fine, but I want twenty percent. Fully healed, her skin alone will fetch enough for both of us to retire on."

I bit down on my tongue to keep from crying out. Yanking my wrists, a tear slid from my eye as I realized they were bound in front of me.

No. No. No.

"I heard the witches like the bones more than the skin," the man said.

The woman scoffed. "I've been doing this over fifty years. Trust me, a freshly-skinned demon fetches no greater price."

Freshly. Skinned. Demon.

Demon?

I screamed then. I mean, if I was going to be skinned alive, I might as well fucking put up a fight, and if I didn't scream, I was going to lose my mind.

The man crossed the room quickly and held up a steel mallet.

Oh God.

"Wait!" the witch cried from the corner. "Don't bash her brain in, I need it whole."

Oh. My. Leaning over, I vomited onto the man's bare feet.

He sighed, looking over at the woman. "Can I wash this off? Or is vomit worth something too?"

The woman scowled at him, stepping out from the shadows. "Everything on this little demon is worth something. You don't pluck a hair from her head without my say so."

He pulled a knife from his belt and nodded. "What should I start with?"

The woman had stepped into the firelight and I could see her more fully now. She was younger than I thought. I mean, she said she'd been doing this for fifty years, but she looked early thirties. Stocky, with thick wavy hair and a harsh face, she wore dirty clothes that looked like they'd been pieced together. Life had not been kind to this woman, I could see that. But on top of that she was...what was she?

I inhaled, confused by her pointy fey ears and yet vampire smell.

She looked right down at me, took in my confused appearance and laughed. The sound made my skin crawl. "You trying to figure it out, love?"

I nodded. Anything to keep her talking and not skinning me alive. Where was Walsh? Was he dead? My memories were fuzzy. The nice Paladin man had tried to help me and then they killed him. Walsh would have seen the dozen hunters and surely turned back for help…right? He'd tell Sawyer and Sawyer would come for me…he wouldn't leave me here.

The woman reached out and grasped me by the hair, pulling me up into a sitting position. I hissed as pain shot up my skull, my wolf coming to the surface; pelts of fur rolled down my arms and I growled.

She grinned. "There you are, little demon." Then she pointed to herself, and the dude standing next to her. "We are *Ith-a-cki.*" She spoke slowly like I was stupid. "Part fey, part other magical creature. It's rare, but sometimes interbreeding with a fey results in pregnancy, and when it does…" She clicked her tongue: "You better flee to the forest, or the fey will kill that baby before it's born." She grinned, showing a missing front tooth. "We're bad luck. Just. Like. *You.*"

My heart pounded in my ears as I processed what she said. The breeds couldn't intermix, or at least that's what I was always told. If a vampire and a werewolf had sex, a child would never result. Just like a dog and a lion couldn't have a baby. But maybe...the fey DNA was closer...like a lion and a tiger.

The Ithaki were...ligers.

Before I could respond, anything to keep her talking, and not cutting, there was a shout of alarm outside.

That's when I heard it.

A pack of wolves.

Thank God.

The woman hissed, her vampire fangs distending onto her bottom lip as the man went to the front of the tent.

"Paladins?" the woman asked.

He shook his head. "They aren't stupid enough to come on our land for a little demon girl. It's a pack of Wolf City wolves."

She cursed. "Get Butcher."

Butcher. Was that a name or a profession? Because I really needed it to be a name...

The man leapt out of the tent as the woman grabbed a pair of pliers from her desk and stalked over to where I sat, hands and ankles bound, leaning up against the wall.

I watched the pliers in her hand as she gripped them in her fist and then reached out lightning-quick and grabbed me by the back of the head.

"Hold still, I just need one eye."

Oh fuck that.

Fear surged up inside of me as my wolf shook my skin like a cage, begging to be freed.

If I died, or lost an eye, these cuffs would be to blame. *Sawyer* would be to blame. I couldn't let that happen. I liked living too much.

I let her get close to me, leaning in to try to take my eye, and that's when I came up with my zip-tied hands, holding both fists balled together, and cracked her so hard under her chin that I heard her teeth break.

She stumbled backward, screaming in pain as I leapt from the fireplace wall and hopped like a bunny across the room. I almost lost my balance as dizziness washed over me, but knew staying upright was my only shot at living. When I reached the door, I threw my shoulder into it and leapt out of the house.

Oh shit.

Many things hit me all at once.

One: this was a tree house. Two: I was falling very rapidly to the ground. And three: Sawyer had just shown up with over thirty wolves, armed to the teeth.

By some trick of fate, the tree house was only about six feet off the ground, maybe to help with flooding or ground insects. There was a pile of freshly raked leaves that I crashed into, softening the blow, and I sent up a quick prayer of thanks to whomever raked them. Still, it hurt. Everything hurt so damn much from my first fall that when I slammed into the leaves a howl ripped from my throat, followed by a whimper.

"Demi!" Sawyer's voice was panicked and raw. As I'd been falling, I'd seen him in human form, coming up the ridge with the others. He must have seen me fall out. I rolled over the bed of leaves and popped back to my feet, jumping again like a bunny, just wanting to get to Sawyer and his men so I could be safe.

He came for me. I knew he'd come for me.

"Look out!" Sawyer yelled, and everything in me tensed as someone grabbed me from behind, their strong hand coming around the back of my throat and a sleek steel knife going to the front.

This person holding me radiated power I could sense and smell. When he pulled me to his chest, I knew it was a different man from the one who had originally kidnapped me.

I was panting, out of breath and out of hope as Sawyer and his wolf pack finally reached us.

Doors slammed and ropes descended from the trees, and suddenly over a hundred Ithaki were gliding down from the tree houses and meeting their leader, who I was one-hundred-percent sure was the man holding a knife to my throat.

Sawyer was wearing a full black camouflage jumpsuit, knives and guns at his waist, and another held loosely in his hand.

The Ithaki held bows and arrows and spears, all aimed at him.

"Let. Her. Go." Sawyer's voice was barely human.

Fur kept trying to erupt from his skin as his wolf tried to take control.

The man behind me laughed. "Finders keepers. You're trespassing, and so was she when we found her. It was all legal, by the book."

Sawyer clenched his jaw. "She fell. She didn't wander. You will release her to me right now and I will pay you for the trouble." Sawyer snapped his fingers and a young male wolf stepped forward with a suitcase, but the knife dug harder into my skin and I yelped.

"You think we want your money? Poisonous *Werewolf City* money?" The man spat behind me.

My eyes flicked to the female vampire-fey; she'd just joined us, holding her hopefully broken jaw and glaring at me.

Sawyer's eyes flashed yellow. "I'm *not* leaving without her. Alive. The alpha has dispatched helicopters, and they will come shortly, laying waste to your entire encampment if you don't release her to me. *Now.*"

The knife cut into my throat and I felt the trickle of blood rush down my chest as I gasped. "Not before I kill her."

Sawyer put his hands up. "Okay, okay! I'll call off the 'copters, just tell me what you *want.*"

I suddenly felt ashamed. It was so stupid of me to fall. Now a Paladin man was killed and Sawyer had dispatched helicopters? What a mess. But I was grateful he was here, fighting for me. He seemed to always show up when I needed him, and that was something I'd grown to love. He was dependable.

"I want you, the alpha's *son*," the man behind me spat, and I flinched.

No.

"I want to fight, like the good old days. Wolf to wolf. Winner gets the money *and* the girl."

So he *did* want the money, but he also wanted to kill Sawyer.

"No!" I growled at the same time that Sawyer started to unbutton his shirt.

"Agreed. Winner takes all." Sawyer didn't look at me, he just took off his shirt and leaned into Walsh, whispering something.

"Sawyer, no!" I shouted. "He's not just a wolf!"

The man behind me laughed. Within a second he'd removed the blade from my throat and tossed me to the vampire-fey, who caught me, and then another blade was pressing against my jugular.

"I know what he is," Sawyer responded, half man, half wolf.

Sawyer was jacked, but I seriously doubted his ability to fight for some reason. He was...too pretty to be a dirty fighter. He was the kind of guy who had bodyguards and could probably shoot someone, but rip their throat out? I just didn't know, and I didn't want him getting killed.

"Don—" I tried to warn him off again and Vampire

Bitch wrestled her hand around my mouth. All I could do was watch helplessly as the crowd surrounding us began to form a circle.

Eugene slowly broke away from the Wolf City pack and weaved his way over to where I was standing with a blade to my throat.

"That's far enough, giant," the woman said to Eugene without looking at him. He was about five feet away now and simply nodded, holding his hands behind his back. My gaze flicked to Eugene and I tried to read if he was worried for Sawyer or not, but he just stood stock still, glaring at the fight about to unfold before us.

The man in the middle of the fight ring had a giant tattoo across his back.

Butcher, it read.

A name...a name after a profession? I prayed I would never find out.

"Do you want to be able to end this fight by forfeit or death only?" Butcher asked Sawyer, sweat gleaming off of his back tattoo.

I tried to glean information from that. Maybe they would be allowed to forfeit and keep their life? That was a nice option and I was glad he was giving Sawyer—

"Death is the only way out of this fight, you sick motherfucker," Sawyer growled and then beat his chest twice like a warrior, before shifting instantly.

Holy shit.

The nice rich boy with polite manners that I'd met

was gone. In his place was some bloodthirsty warrior who I was *extremely* attracted to right now. I probably needed therapy for these thoughts, but seeing Sawyer turn into a bloodthirsty wolf, lips curled back in a snarl, it...pulled my heart back in his direction. Any anger I'd had at him for locking these cuffs on me was gone. I could see now that he was just being protective of me, that in his mind, these cuffs made me safe, even if now they would get me killed. He would do anything to protect me, that was clear now.

Butcher shifted as well, and I was pleased to see his wolf was much smaller than Sawyer's, but I had no idea what fey powers he might have in his wolf form. Hybrids were not talked about. The two wolves stalked each other in a slow circle, hackles of each wolf rising as they bared their teeth at each other, saliva glistening off of the white sharp points.

Butcher's wolf dove and I sucked in a breath, but Sawyer rolled out of the way.

He was fast.

Really fast.

Sawyer popped up onto his feet and shook the dirt from his fur as Butcher lunged again. Sawyer's wolf kicked off the ground and soared over Butcher's head, landing on the other side and avoiding being bitten.

I internally cheered, afraid that if I spoke, the Ithaki with the knife to my throat would kill me.

Butcher just looked pissed now that he realized he

was unable to catch his prey. He lunged three more times in rapid succession and Sawyer dodged every single one.

He was so damn fast, vampire-fast, and I could see his strategy now was a strong evasive defense rather than offensively attacking. Sawyer looked barely winded while Butcher was panting like an out-of-shape dog. Butcher was doing all the hard work and heavy lifting and he hadn't even grazed Sawyer yet.

Maybe I'd misjudged Sawyer's fighting ability; he was clearly trained.

The air charged then, something that was hard to explain, but it felt thick and full of static electricity. For a second I wondered if I was the only one who felt it, but Sawyer's fur stood up on end and he lowered his ears as if he was in pain.

Butcher's wolf grinned, a slight blue mist lifting off of his skin.

Fey magic?

I wanted to move, to rush forward and help, but the knife at my throat tightened, and I was helpless with these stupid cuffs on. Sawyer whined, ears flat to his head as an ultrasonic noise picked up throughout the space. Every wolf in attendance winced, covering their ears with their hands, or flattening their ears if in wolf form. It felt like my brain was going to explode; my ears would start bleeding any moment. I wanted to reach up and cover them, but with a knife to my throat I just gritted my teeth and bore it.

Butcher lunged then and Eugene stepped forward to the very edge of the fight ring, "Tokyo!" he screamed at Sawyer, who shook himself before rearing up on his hind legs and catching Butcher's wolf mid-attack.

Tokyo?

Did I hear that right?

Butcher slammed into Sawyer, who wrapped his front paws over the Ithaki's shoulders and they snapped jaws at each other's faces viciously.

The ultrasonic sound magic had stopped and I wondered if Butcher wasn't able to do that and attack at the same time. Maybe the fey magic took too much concentration. Either way, it didn't matter, because he was able to finally catch Sawyer, and now they were locked in one of the worst fights I'd ever seen. The *only* wolf fight I'd ever seen, but still. Sawyer grazed Butcher's muzzle, raking his teeth along the skin and tearing it open as fresh *purple* blood oozed from the cut.

Purple?

Whoa.

Fey blood was blue, my mom told me, and wolf blood was red. Purple Ithaki hybrid blood.

I was so enthralled in what I was seeing that I'd lost sight of the fight. Only when the sound of crunching bone cut through the space and the Ithaki present started to roar in triumph did I drag my gaze to Sawyer.

"No!" I screamed as Butcher tore into Sawyer's

flank, ripping away a piece of flesh and exposing his ribs. Sawyer howled, long and hauntingly deep.

"Morocco!" Eugene yelled and Sawyer collapsed to the ground, panting as fresh crimson blood oozed from the wound. He tried to stand, but fell back down.

Morocco?

They must have had a secret playbook of fights or something. I felt more and more like I was watching a college football game with a coach on the sidelines.

Oh God no. I couldn't even focus on the fact that Eugene was shouting random countries and cities at Sawyer, I could only focus on the fact that it looked like Sawyer was down and couldn't get up.

"Get up, Sawyer!" I yelled and the vampire-fey yanked my hair back painfully, causing me to wince. Butcher circled Sawyer like a shark stalking his victim. Sawyer snapped out at him a few times, but every time he tried to get up, he slipped and fell back down.

I couldn't...couldn't look, but I also couldn't look away. Sawyer came here for me, he'd agreed to fight for me, and now he was going to die for me, and I was going to watch.

Butcher leapt, going for the throat, the kill, and everything inside of me seized up.

No. No. No.

My first thought was that I didn't get to kiss this guy enough, I never got to love him, I really wanted to have more time with him, I wasn't done.

Sawyer watched Butcher lunge, almost with an expression of resigned fate, but as Butcher grew nearer, I saw Sawyer's muscles tighten. When he was nearly on top of him, Sawyer rolled, letting Butcher have the upper hand and pin him underneath his body.

This was it.

I steeled myself, ready to watch Butcher rip Sawyer's throat out, but…it never came. The moment Butcher landed on Sawyer, he kicked up with all four paws and bucked him off, sending him flying through the air. Then Sawyer clambered to his feet with surprising agility and strength and stalked across the space like a cheetah.

"Paris!" Eugene yelled, and one of the Ithaki nearest Eugene kicked the back of his knee out, sending him crashing to the ground, the word dying in this throat. It had now become very clear to everyone here that Eugene and Sawyer were a team. Sawyer had clearly trained for these types of fights and Eugene was directing the show.

Butcher had landed hard when Sawyer kicked him off, and he was still struggling to get up. He probably had some broken ribs too. Sawyer tore across the space so fast and even with a slight limp, he was on Butcher in seconds. That electric charge filtered through the air again and that ultrasonic painful sound ripped through the space, but it was lesser this time, frantic and uncoordinated. Sawyer's wolf flinched, but dove for the kill anyway. The entire crowd that had assembled held their collective breath as Sawyer wrapped his teeth around

Butcher's jugular and clamped down with a sickening crunch. He jerked his head to the side and came away with a chunk of flesh. Butcher's body jerked, spraying purple blood in a high arc, and then he went still.

Holy shifter.

The knife at my throat tightened, began to cut into my skin, and then a gunshot cut through the space and the knife fell away as the vampire-fey dropped to the ground behind me. Eugene stood five paces away, sleek black gun raised.

My legs were suddenly too weak to hold me. The fall down the mountain and the fall out of the tree had injured me so badly I wasn't sure how I'd stayed standing this entire time.

"We've met the requirements of your demands and we *will* be taking the girl," Eugene called out to the people, who looked shocked at their dead leader on the ground. "We will leave the money for any inconvenience we've caused you."

A helicopter whirred overhead and people started to back up, holding their spears to the sky as if they'd never seen a helicopter before.

Maybe they hadn't.

Eugene reached me, cutting my hand and leg bindings, and everything spun as the last drop of adrenaline left me.

I was saved. I wasn't going to be skinned alive. Sawyer won his fight.

I started to fall forward when a blur of dark hair flashed before me and Sawyer caught me right before I hit the ground. His strong arms scooped under my knees and behind my back, hauling me against his chest. Warm, tight, safe arms cradled me so hard it actually hurt. My cuts and bruises weren't healing like a shifter's should, and I winced as Sawyer loosened his hold.

"Oh God, Demi. I'm so fucking sorry," he murmured against me, the warmth of his breath feathering over my face as my chest tightened.

Eugene approached him. "Sawyer, you're badly hurt. I can carry her."

His response was a guttural growl and Eugene dropped his head in response, giving Sawyer the top of his head in a submissive gesture.

Sawyer walked me to the helicopter and called out over his shoulder, screaming over the whirring blades. "Get me a witch to get these fucking cuffs off of her!"

When he looked down at me, his blue eyes held so much anguish, so much regret, it broke my heart. "Can you ever forgive me?" His voice cracked and he looked genuinely panicked that I would say no.

I'd never met a guy like Sawyer, one who was so intense and protective, and one that asked forgiveness for his mistakes. I had to be honest with myself here, this was an all or nothing moment in our budding relationship. I either said yes and we moved forward in the direction of where we were going, or I said no and probably cause irreversible harm to any future we might have had.

Honestly? I'd never had a man fight for me like Sawyer did. From day one he'd been in my corner. And people made mistakes.

"Yes."

I forgave him. I forgave him for thinking that hiding what I was would protect me. It obviously wouldn't. We were going to have to come up with a plan B, together. With a deep sigh, he rested his forehead against mine and everything inside of me opened to him. I realized I'd been keeping a wall up, something to protect me in case he chose another girl, but now I was all in. I wanted to win his heart and in order to do that, I needed to lower all of my defenses.

"I'm going to make this up to you," he whispered as we climbed into the chopper. Everything hurt, my skin, my bones, my muscles, everything.

"Thanks for coming to save me," I told him.

He shook his head and swallowed hard. "It's the least I could do after *you* saved me."

I frowned. A medic started to look at a gash on my elbow and his words pinged around in my head.

How did I save him? Maybe this had to do with the brokenness I saw inside of him the day we met, the heaviness in his deep blue eyes that sometimes came to the surface to signal that he was dealing with too much.

"You're going to need surgery," the medic said to

Sawyer. "A skin graft, and then your healing should take over from there."

He shook his head. "No. I'll be fine."

The medic, a blond female about thirty, frowned. "It will scar, and it will take days to heal."

He looked at her with hard eyes. "I'm not leaving her side." The wolf threaded into his voice and the woman lowered her gaze.

"Sawyer—" another medic said, but his wolf was out, there would be no reasoning with him and that was obvious. Eugene jumped into the helicopter and we took flight.

"Witch is on the way. Will meet us at your place. I thought you might like to be discreet," Eugene told Sawyer.

He nodded. "And call Doctor Berns to look over Demi. He can meet us at my apartment too."

Eugene's eyes widened. "Your father's private doctor is for the alpha family only. I don't think—"

"I wasn't *asking*, Eugene." Sawyer's voice was short and clipped.

With a nod, Eugene dialed another number and I reached out to stroke Sawyer's face, pulling him down to look at me. His eyes were blazing yellow. I was guessing his wolf didn't like being in such a small space with other people and a bad injury, but I knew his wolf was also protective over me. More than human Sawyer was.

"I'm okay. You did good, and I'm okay now," I purred into his ear, trying to soothe his wolf.

He held up my arm, putting the cuff in full view of my face. "*Nothing* about this is okay." His voice cracked with emotion. "I basically left you human, you could have been—"

"But I'm not." I ran my thumb over his bottom lip and he shuddered, eyes flashing yellow to blue and then back to yellow.

"I fucked up. Demi, I'm so sorry I fucked up." His grip around me tightened and I winced because it hurt my injuries a little, but at the same time I needed it. I needed him, I wanted to be closer. I couldn't get enough of this feeling that he provided when he held me.

I felt safe.

I felt adored.

I felt like I was falling in love.

All of it scared the shit out of me and filled the holes inside of me at the same time.

"Shhh," I soothed in his ear. "I forgive you."

He nodded, his dark hair splashing across his forehead. "Never again." He tapped the cuff. "Never again."

And I believed him.

CHAPTER THIRTEEN

"I NEED YOU TO LAY HER ON THE BED, SAWYER." A TALL man in a white doctor's coat peered at Sawyer with a slight look of alarm. Sawyer hadn't let me down since we left the Wild Lands. He'd held me to his chest in the helicopter. He'd carried me through campus into his house. And now a bunch of dominant males wanted to examine me and his wolf was back, glaring at the men with yellow eyes.

The bed had been stripped and covered in plastic sheeting, then a white gauzy linen. We didn't go to his old house where the vampires attacked like I thought we would; he must have moved after that incident. We were in a giant glass house that was slightly more off campus but surrounded by open green grass and men with machine guns monitoring the perimeter.

He just glared at the doctor, chest heaving, arms snuggled tightly around me.

"Sawyer..." I pulled his face to mine and met that blazing yellow gaze. "I'm in pain and I'd like the doctor to help me. I had a really bad fall down the mountain. I need you to put me down."

His eyes bled into blue and his face contorted in agony, as if thinking of me in pain caused him to also feel discomfort.

With a nod, he lay me on the bed and then hovered six inches over me.

The doctor cleared his throat. "I need *space* to examine her."

With a growl, Sawyer pushed off the bed and stood behind the doctor and his female assistant and they immediately went to work.

The female clicked her tongue as she pulled up my shirt to look at my stomach. "Does it hurt when you breathe in deeply?" she asked.

I looked down at the purple splotching bruises on my ribcage and nodded. I'd been taking shallow breaths this entire time.

"*Broken ribs*," the doctor typed into his tablet.

I could hear Sawyer's jaw clamp shut from here; his teeth clacked together. He started to pace the room as they continued to inspect me. Flashing a light in my eyes, they had me follow their finger.

"Concussion," the doctor said.

"Motherfuckers!" Sawyer growled and the doctor flinched but carried on.

The doctor inspected my bleeding and crusted elbow. "She'll need sutures for this laceration on the elbow."

The woman frowned. "Why isn't she healing?"

Sawyer's growl turned into a whine. "Where's the witch!" he cried into the hallway. "Get these fucking cuffs off her!"

Eugene's voice came back: "She's on her way."

The two doctors shared a look, and then Sawyer swallowed hard. "Her...the cuffs basically make her human. She can't heal until they come off." There was so much gut-wrenching guilt in his tone that it brought tears to my eyes. I reached out a hand for him but he faced the wall, head down as if he couldn't even look at me in that moment.

The woman raised her eyebrows but said nothing while the male doctor let his eyes roam over Sawyer's naked back. "Let me look at that nasty wound on your flank."

"I'm fine," Sawyer growled, spinning back around with yellow eyes. "Demi first."

The doctor shook his head. "I can see your ribcage, Sawyer. Werewolves are not impervious to infection, my duty is to the alpha fami—"

"Your duty is to follow orders." Sawyer looked murderous, and I just wanted to fall asleep, everything felt so heavy. "Help. Demi. *First.* She is my family."

She is my family.

Were there ever four more powerful words? I wondered if I'd even heard him right.

The doctor sighed and rubbed the back of his neck.

"I'll need to get a CT on her. And I'd like to x-ray her spine and ribs," he ordered, and the woman typed up something on her tablet. "Even if we can get her healing back, she'll heal all wrong and have a permanent injury without the bones being set properly."

Oh God.

I tried to focus on his words but everything in the room spun and I started to feel nauseated.

"I feel sick," I told them both.

They shared a look. "Could be a brain bleed. Order that CT scan stat, and where is this witch? We need those cuffs off now before damage begins to become permanent," the doctor barked to the female and Sawyer simultaneously.

Sawyer fell to his knees, leaning over me at the bed, his face contorted into absolute misery. "Demi?" His voice was a hoarse whisper, fading in and out with warbled tones.

"Hmm?" I tried to focus on staying awake, but everything was too bright. Too loud. Too heavy.

Leaning in, he whispered in my ear. "I don't deserve you." His breath feathered over me. "But I don't think I can live without you...assuming you'll even have me." My brain was too slow in trying to process those words. Everything felt so heavy and sluggish and loud and painful.

Did Sawyer just...I couldn't think any more about

it because a tide of black water yanked me under and everything drifted away.

When I came to, I felt warmth beneath my cheek. Then the rise and fall of someone's chest. Cracking open my eyes, I let the sunlight filter in and looked up. Two burning blue eyes stared down at me.

"How are you feeling?" Sawyer's arms wrapped around me tighter, as if he were afraid I was going to run away.

I took in a deep breath and felt no pain. My eyes flicked down to my wrists—no cuffs.

Oh thank God. My wolf stirred at the thought of freedom.

"I'm okay." I tried to sit up and there was a moment when Sawyer held on, not letting me go, but then it passed and I pulled myself up to a sitting position as he released me.

We were silent, just looking at each other, unsure what to say. My eyes ran over a bandage at his ribcage. "You okay?"

He shook his head. "My wolf. I...when I heard the Ithaki took you—" He sighed, running his hands over his face. "I need to tell you something, Demi."

My heart hammered in my chest. I'd forgotten all about his promise to give me answers, to tell me what he knew about me or whatever it was he seemed to be hiding. We were supposed to have some romantic dinner where he cooked for me. Sage had some surprise. Everything got messed up. I didn't even know what day it was. I'd clearly had some kind of procedure, because my right foot was in a walking boot.

"They called me a demon." I frowned. "The Ithaki."

He nodded. "They think split shifters are demons. They say that whatever caused your soul to split is too dark to be allowed to live."

My throat went bone dry as I thought back to my rape. Is that when it happened? I blacked out and when I'd woken up...

My mouth popped open. The attack on the vampires who assaulted me...they'd said it looked like they'd been mauled by a bear or wolf, but what if...it was *me*? What if my wolf split off to protect me? With the cuffs on, was that even possible?

I was so in shock that I'd forgotten Sawyer was speaking. "The Ithaki are monsters. They harvest organs, capture animals and torture them for their essence and sell everything to the Danai."

I frowned. "Danai?"

He nodded. "A band of seriously dark and evil witches who live in the Wild Lands."

Dawning shone in my eyes. Raven used to speak of them but never said their name. She went all Harry Potter and just called them "the nameless."

He got quiet and reached out to touch my cheek. "What happened to make your soul split?"

I stilled, swallowing hard. I should probably tell him, especially if we were going to be intimate, and I had no idea how I would react to sex after my attack. I blew out a shaky breath and—

Someone pounded on the door.

"Sawyer!" It was his mother. My eyes widened as I realized we were in his bed together, him with his shirt off.

Soooo not appropriate.

"Open the door, son!" his father growled.

"Shit," I hissed, and jumped up, but then winced as I realized I came down on my walking boot and my ankle throbbed.

Sawyer's eyes widened. "Whoa. Go easy. Why don't you take a relaxing shower and I'll get rid of them? Then we can have some breakfast brought over and talk some more?"

I nodded and the banging got louder. "Sawyer James Hudson!" his mother roared. "Did you fight the *Ithaki* last night? Open this door right now!"

He groaned and then stood, looking back at me. "Don't worry about them knowing you're here. It's not a big deal, they know how I feel about you."

They know how I feel about you?

I just nodded and slipped into his bathroom, shutting the door behind me and resting my head against it.

Muffled shouting made its way back to me as his father's voice filtered through the room. "I go out of town for one day and you kill the Ithaki *leader*?"

"He kidnapped Demi, was five seconds from skinning her alive," Sawyer growled.

"Oh fate." His mother gasped. "Why...why would they want Demi?"

Silence.

"She fell. Who knows. The Ithaki are sick. They'll do anything to make a few bucks from the Danai."

Oh. I'd forgotten for a second that he didn't tell his parents about my...issues. No longer wanting to hear this conversation, I started to run the shower.

Looking at the countertop, I grinned when I saw a brand-new toothbrush, floral girly coconut shampoo and conditioner, and even fresh new clothes. Sawyer was so thoughtful.

I stripped out of my bloody, dirty, disgusting clothes, pausing when I remembered my walking boot.

Ugh.

Slowly peeling the Velcro straps back, I slipped a purple bruised foot out of the boot and then hobbled into the shower, careful not to bear weight on the healing ankle. When I looked down at the blood-splattered, purple-blotched skin of my naked body, tears formed in my eyes.

Holy shit.

That was so close. I almost died. I tried not to think

about falling down that fucking mountain, Walsh running after me, and the sweet Paladin man who tried to help me before the Ithaki killed him. Shaking the thoughts from my head, I started to soap up, watching the red and brown-tinged water pool at my feet as I scrubbed clean. I wanted to stay in here forever and not deal with telling Sawyer I was raped, but it was time to get all this shit out there, especially if I was serious about being with him.

I quickly brushed my teeth, slipped into the new clothes, including the walking boot, and towel dried my long blond hair. Then I stepped out of the room and froze.

"Sawyer, are you sure? If we call off the mating selection and she's not the one—"

"She's the *one*," he growled, and my stomach bottomed out. A huge grin swept across my face and I wanted to run out there and jump into his arms, but I was totally snooping so I stayed where I was.

"Meredith is a safe bet," his mother said, and the grin fled from my face.

"I don't love Meredith."

There was a deep long sigh as his mother seemingly weighed his words. "You don't have to love them back, son. Our entire family is depending on you—"

"I'd like you to go now, Mother. I've made my choice. It's Demi, it's *always* been her."

Holy shit.

This conversation was so confusing but I didn't care. The only part that mattered was that Sawyer basically just said he chose me.

"If you're sure, I'll call for an early announcement in a few days' time." She sounded dejected.

"Thank you," Sawyer responded, annoyance in his voice.

The clipped sound of high heels fled down the hallway and then the front door shut.

"You can come out now," Sawyer spoke into the room and I flinched. How did he know I was there? Hopefully his mom didn't.

I stepped out gingerly, limping on the walking boot, and Sawyer let his gaze rake up and down my body. It wasn't his usual hungry gaze. He was searching for wounds.

He tipped his head to the door. "Did you hear all that?"

I shrugged. "Just the part about you choosing me... no big deal."

A slow grin pulled at his mouth and he stepped closer to me and released a shaky breath. "From the moment I first saw you...I knew you were *mine*."

It was like time stopped; my breathing definitely did; and maybe even my heart too. I think I actually died for a minute when he said it. It wasn't in a possessive way, it was just matter of fact, like we were made for each other.

I swallowed hard and he stepped closer. "Well, my wolf knew. I didn't want to freak you out, and I'm not sure if you feel the same because you and your wolf are so separate…" His face faltered. "Come to think of it, I'm probably freaking you out right now." He ran a nervous hand through his hair. "I, uh…I dunno, Demi, I just…what I'm trying to say is—"

I cut his words off with a kiss, pressing my body flat against his, and was rewarded with a moan. His fingers gently came around the back of my neck to cradle my head as my lips parted and our tongues slid against each other. Sawyer thought my wolf and I were separate, and in a way we were, but I'd felt the same from day one about him, I just never wanted to admit it. Survival instinct, or whatever you want to call it, I just didn't want to get hurt. Knowing that he felt the same, it smashed every wall I had built.

His hand trailed up the back of my shirt and I raked my fingers down his back, causing him to freeze. He pulled away and looked down at me and I frowned.

"What's wrong? Did I hurt you?" I asked.

He shook his head. "No, I just…we need to talk about something. Can you come sit down?" He pulled away from me, taking the heat of his body with him, and I frowned.

Damn. This was not what I expected we'd be doing right now after he all but declared his love for me.

Talking.

I sat on the couch next to him and he faced me, mouth in a hard line, eyes distant. His brokenness was close to the surface, and I knew whatever it was, it would be bad. But I wouldn't judge him for it, Lord knew I had my own issues.

"I don't know how to say this, it's been a secret for so long...I don't even know how to vocalize it."

Okay...I was getting more scared by the moment. "Just tell me." Because I was imagining the worst. *He's already mated and has a kid. He can't marry me because of what I am. Out with it!* I wanted to shake him, but it was clear he needed a moment.

"There's...there's a curse over my family," he breathed, and I frowned. That was not what I was expecting him to say.

"Okay, like how?" Did he turn into an ogre at midnight, because not gonna lie, that would suck.

He chewed his bottom lip. "Sage doesn't even know this, okay? It's like *top* secret. I'm only supposed to tell the woman I choose on our wedding night."

Whoa. The entire atmosphere in the room shifted and everything felt really scary all of a sudden. "Sawyer, just tell me, I'm freaking out."

He grabbed my hands. "Okay, sorry, I mean, it's not *that* big of a deal. Just...about a thousand years ago my great-great-great-great grandfather pissed off a Danai witch and she cursed our entire family line."

I nodded, needing him to get on with what the actual

curse was! My mind ran wild with fairy tales I'd heard as a kid. Did he turn into a frog? Would he die on his thirtieth birthday? *What?*

He swallowed hard. "By my twenty-third birthday, I have to find a wife to marry me who actually loves me for me."

He breathed out like he had been holding in too much air.

I frowned. "Wait...what? You just have to marry someone that loves you? Okay...that's easy. Obviously half the school loves you. I mean, twenty-three is a bit young but—"

He nodded. "A millennium ago, that was actually pretty old, but no, Demi, you don't understand. If I pick the wrong girl and she likes me for my money or status or whatever, then the curse...it kills my entire family line."

I froze, shaking my head. "Say what now?"

He released his hands and stood, starting to pace the floor. "This is so fucking awkward."

I stood, hobbling across the space and stepping in front of him. "No it's fine, I'm just...processing. So, *everyone* dies if you marry the wrong girl?"

He nodded. "Every Hudson. My mom, my dad, me, Sage, my uncle. They all drop dead as the curse is unleashed and takes out our line forever."

"Holy shit," I gasped. "That's seriously awful. And it just goes on forever and ever?"

He nodded. "The alpha's wife is cursed with only being able to have two sons. My uncle, not being the alpha because he was the youngest, was able to have Sage, but..."

Dawning came over me. I'd put on the questionnaire that I wanted twin girls. "Wow, that's quite a complex curse." This ancient witch really thought of everything. Two sons, but you—" I paused, seeing sadness in his face.

"I was a twin actually. My brother was a stillborn." His voice cracked and my heart broke.

"I'm so sorry." I took his hand as my mind processed everything he was saying. "So this entire selection, it's all just so that you can keep your family alive?"

He winced. "When you put it that way it sounds bad...but yes, it's so that I can find at least one girl who *truly* loves me. That's why I kept Meredith around...she was always a safe bet."

I growled, suddenly jealous. "Meredith doesn't love you. She's obsessed with you. There's a difference."

His eyes flashed yellow and he pulled me closer to him. "If I don't find someone who truly loves me to marry me by the end of next year, then my entire family dies."

I frowned. "So this is your darkness?"

"What?"

"When we first met, I saw a darkness in your soul, a heaviness you carried. This is it."

He nodded. "I guess it is."

"Wait, so you don't have to love the person back?" The wheels started to turn in my head as I realized why he spoke of Meredith. It was clear he didn't love her, but if she loved him, then he'd still marry her.

He shook his head. "No. But I don't just want to be loved, I want to be *in* love."

This was why he told Sage he was worried about finding someone to love him. He felt pressure to keep his family alive. Damn, that was quite a weight to carry.

I stepped closer to him. "What if you don't find someone you love? Will you just choose Meredith to be safe?"

A slow grin pulled across his face. "I thought I just covered that, Demi. I'm in love with *you*."

The breath whooshed out of me like a kick in the gut. He said it so casually, so sure. I'd never met a man with so much confidence. He knew what he wanted and he didn't fuck around going after it. That was why his mom was so worried if I was the one. Her life *depended* on me loving Sawyer back. Loving her son for the guy he was, not the Hudson heir or the alpha's son.

Good thing she raised a gentleman, because the next six words were the easiest I'd ever said. "I'm in love with you too." I laughed. "Holy shit, this is wild. I barely know you but I lov—" He crashed into me and captured my mouth in a kiss. My entire stomach did somersaults as he gripped my ass, hauling me onto him so that I was straddling him. My breath was ragged as he feathered my neck with kisses, trailing his tongue along my collarbone, and passion completely took over me. I grinded into him when he nipped my earlobe and heat exploded between my legs.

Sawyer walked us back to the bedroom and lay me gently on the bed, kissing my forehead. "I went mad when I heard you'd been taken." He leaned down and pulled up my shirt, kissing my stomach. "I nearly killed Walsh for leaving you." His hand slipped up my shirt, grasped my breast and all rational thought left me.

I should have stuck up for Walsh, who'd probably saved my life by getting help, but I couldn't think. All I could think about was how badly I needed to be closer to Sawyer. I sat up and Sawyer backed off, watching me as I slowly pulled my shirt up and over my head. He watched me as I gradually unclipped my bra and his eyes went yellow.

With a grin, he grabbed my hands, laying me back down, and pinned them over my head. Slight panic flooded my system and I didn't understand why. It was in such direct contrast to how I wanted to feel in this moment. When Sawyer placed his mouth over my nipple and sucked, keeping my hands pinned above me, I understood why.

"Let go!" I half shouted, trying to yank my hands free as a flashback hit me.

Sawyer immediately jumped off of me, looking down

at me apologetically as I tried to drown out the vision of Vicon Drake pinning my arms above me and biting my breast, drinking from it.

"Shit, did I go too far? I'm sorry I just—"

Tears lined my eyes as I put on my t-shirt and then covered my face with my hands. I'd slept with one guy, Isaac the fey, after my virginity was stolen by rape, and it was *so* fucking awkward. I was so eager to prove to myself that I was sexually normal after my attack that I just lay there and prayed it would pass quickly. It did.

"I can't be held down," I told him, my face still in my hands.

Two warm hands grasped my forearms and peeled them away from my face, until I was staring at yellow eyes. "Did someone hurt you, Demi?" His voice was that scary half wolf growl.

I swallowed hard, releasing a deep sigh. "It's my turn to tell you something." I pulled my arms out of his and patted the bed.

His entire body was tense, jaw clenched as he sat next to me. "You can tell me anything. But first, are you okay? Did I hurt you?"

The fact that he was being so sweet just made those half unshed tears pour over. "I'm fine, you *didn't* hurt me. This is...an old emotional pain that resurfaced."

He was silent, still, unreadable other than the yellow eyes that kept peeking out behind his lashes.

It was on the tip of my tongue, but I wasn't ready,

so I just sat there, trying not to think about that night. Other than Raven and my mom and dad, no one knew my story. It was something we all covered up at my request and tried to move on from. Sometimes burying old wounds worked and sometimes they rose up like zombies waking from the dead.

Finally, when I couldn't take it anymore, I spoke. "When I was fifteen, I went to a party in Vampire City..." I breathed.

His eyebrows rose like that was impossible and I nodded. "My best friend Raven and I snuck out with a vampire girl at Delphi and we went to a party with older guys."

Those yellow eyes were back as he sat rigid next to me. "What happened?" he growled, but I knew that the anger wasn't at me, it was at what he knew was about to come out of my mouth in the next sentence.

"I was gang raped by four vampires and left for dead—" I didn't even finish my sentence before the splitting of seams ripped through the space and Sawyer shifted into his wolf. His clothes tore to tatters as his giant gray wolf landed on all fours and looked up at me with pained yellow eyes. Tears streamed down my face as his wolf leapt up from the ground and nuzzled my neck, placing his paws on my shoulders like a hug.

A soft wolfie hug.

A sob escaped me as I wrapped my arms around his giant furry wolf and held him closely. "I think that's when my soul split. The cuffs, they kept me human, so I couldn't fight back." I tried to breathe to calm myself down, but my throat felt so tight as his wolf draped across my body like a blanket and I held him. "I don't remember it. I mean I do, but in flashes, the before, a little of the during, and then way after. There was so much blood, three of the four guys were killed…it looked like an animal had attacked them, but now…" A cry ripped from my throat. "I think that my wolf somehow broke free and saved my life." I had held this in for so long that now that it was out, I couldn't stop the floodgates. "She *saved* me," I wept, "and that's why I am this way, that's why I'm broken."

I squeezed his wolf so tightly I was afraid I would break his ribs and reinjure him, but he just lay on top of me like a loyal animal therapy dog or something and let me get it all out. When he realized I was done, he licked the tears from my cheeks and I laughed. "Gross."

He pushed off of me and started to shift back and I suddenly was nervous about seeing Sawyer in his human form after divulging all that. Telling a soft fluffy wolf your darkest secret was a lot different that a six-foot-six-inch-tall Adonis. Sawyer turned away and I caught a glimpse of his naked butt as he walked into his closet. He returned with basketball shorts and a t-shirt on.

When he reached me, I avoided eye contact as he fell to his knees before me. He was patient, waiting until I looked at him, and when I did I was shocked at the anger I saw in his eyes. I frowned, and he reached out and brushed a finger over my cheek. "*Nothing* about you is broken."

The tears were back as I realized I'd waited for a man I loved to hear my story and tell me that.

I just nodded.

"And in the future, I will let *you* take the lead in the bedroom," he said, but his words didn't match his blazing gaze and steel jaw.

"What's wrong?" I asked, suddenly wondering if he was mad at me.

Sawyer stood. "I'm going to need the name of the guy left alive from that night, Demi."

My mouth popped open. "What? No wa—"

Sawyer's chest started to heave up and down, fur running down his arms. "I'm *going* to need that name, Demi. *Now.*"

The bossy alpha was back. I stood and so did he as I butted my chest up against his. "My parents filed a complaint with Vampire City, but they said since I was banished I had no protection."

Sawyer fled from the room and then there was a crashing noise in the living room.

Holy shit, this man had a temper.

I hobbled out to see that he'd kicked the coffee table in half. It lay in a splintered wood pile at his feet. He looked up at me, barely holding on to his humanity. "Demi, I need that name before I go and light the entirety of Vampire City on fire!"

My eyes nearly fell out of my head. "Sawyer, it was six years ago—"

"Name!" He fisted his hands and they shook. I'd seen my father like this once in my life. The night I told him and my mom about my assault. He'd barely been able to keep his wolf inside, even with the cuffs on.

"Fine! It was Vicon Drake, okay!" I screamed, and he went very still.

He raised one eyebrow. "*Prince* Vicon Drake?"

I nodded once. "I didn't know that at the time, but yeah."

They'd gotten Raven so drunk she'd passed out in the basement, but the boys were stupid enough to brag to us all about their rich and powerful families.

"I'm a Drake, I can get away with murder," he'd said earlier that night after telling me his first name was Vicon. Only later, when my parents had made the formal complaint, did I find out he was prince to the coven that ruled the entire city.

Sawyer grasped me by the arms and leaned in to kiss me chastely. "Call Sage and have her sleep over. I'll put Eugene on the front door, with the rest of my guys walking the perimeter."

I shook my head. "What?"

He released me and started to walk to the door, gray fur rolling down his back. When he reached the door, he looked over his shoulder at me with yellow eyes. "I might be gone for a few days. Just go to class, pretend like everything is normal, but sleep at my place with Sage. It's safest."

"What are you saying? Where are you going?"

Sawyer's jaw clenched. "The only person who should have survived that night is you, Demi." Then he slipped out into the daylight like he didn't just drop a hint that he was going to attempt to murder Prince Vicon Drake.

Oh fuck. That's not how I saw that conversation going.

CHAPTER FOURTEEN

THREE DAYS. SAWYER HAD BEEN MIA FOR *THREE days*. I'd been forced to tell Sage about my attack six years ago, because she was wondering why we were sleeping at Sawyer's and he was gone. He must have told his parents, because they didn't issue a missing persons alert; everything was just very quiet. I went to class, I ate lunch. I looked normal on the outside but inside there was a war going on. Where was he? Was he safe? Did he kill Vicon? Or maybe he was just going to mess him up a little, or scare him by leaving dead rabbits on his bed or something. Yeah…but then I remembered when he said that I was the only person who should have survived that night and fuck. I couldn't sleep very well or eat very much, I just wanted to know he was okay. All I knew was that Walsh was missing too and there was comfort in the fact that he wasn't alone.

The females on campus were a ball of nerves as well. The day after Sawyer left it was announced that he'd chosen his future mate and wife early, and would be announcing it this weekend at a special ceremony. I hadn't really put two and two together and realized that by picking me we had to get married…or his entire family would *die*.

No fucking pressure.

Basically it was just another Wednesday.

I tapped my foot, finally all healed and sans walking boot, as Sage chewed a fingernail.

"He said a few days. It's been three," I whispered.

Sage nodded, leaning into the table. "He's probably staked out where that asshole lives, where he works, stolen a key card so he can get into his place of residence without breaking in…it's a lot of work to covertly assassinate vampire royalty."

My eyes widened and I blinked at her a few times. "You think he really is going to…kill him?"

Sage scoffed. "Only one hundred and fifty percent."

Okay, okay…that was…I mean, did I want that raping asshole to live and do this to another girl? No. But killing him…it was dangerous, and Sawyer was basically royalty too, so if he got caught…

My voice shook: "Why didn't he just send a team or something?"

Sage raised an eyebrow. "Sawyer is in love with you, Demi. He's not going to send a team to enact revenge and fight for your honor, he'll want to do that himself." She laid a hand over mine. "Besides, his wolf has probably taken over anyway. All rational thought is gone."

Oh great.

Fuck.

I'd told Sage that he'd confessed his love for me but not about the curse. I also hadn't told her that I was some freak split shifter. Now that my cuffs were off again, I wondered if my smell, or whatever attracted the vampires to me in the first place, was sending a beacon that said "kidnap me and drain my blood."

"Holy shit," Sage whisper-screamed and pointed to the cafeteria door. Walsh and Sawyer had just walked in, backpacks slung around their shoulders like it was just another school day. Sawyer scanned the tables, and when he saw me he broke into a grin and walked over.

My heart thumped in my throat as he casually sat next to me and pulled a tater tot off my plate, popping it into his mouth.

"Uhhh, hey," I said.

"Hey." He smiled like he was happy, and he hadn't been missing for three days.

Sage cleared her throat. "So...did you, uh, do that thing?"

Walsh and Sawyer shared a look, both grinning. "We had a wonderfully productive hunting trip, thank you for asking."

Hunting trip.

Oh my God...he killed Vicon Drake.

The eight a.m. bell dinged and everyone around us stood. Sawyer leaned into my ear and whispered, "He's never going to hurt you again, Demi. Or anyone else." Then pulled back and tucked a few strands of blond hair behind my ear. "I'll see you tonight?"

All I could do was nod. I guess when an alpha werewolf was in love with you, killing your attacker was a normal thing I would have to get used to.

"Nope. I have that surprise for Demi, remember?" Sage widened her eyes at him in a knowing, conspiratorial look.

Sawyer nodded, giving her a smile.

My brows drew together. "What is this surprise?"

Sawyer and Sage shared a look, and knowing smiles, but said nothing.

"It's just a little something to make you happy. It was supposed to happen the day you went to the waterfall but..."

Yeah, that turned into a shit show.

"Well...I look forward to said surprise." Not really, I hated surprises, but if it was from the two of them, I was sure I'd love it.

I stood, and Sawyer leaned down to grab my backpack, handing it to me like a gentlemen. I noticed Meredith and a few others glaring daggers from the table nearby.

"See you...later." I shifted awkwardly, and half waved to Sawyer.

With a halfcocked smirk, he leaned forward and grabbed the back of my neck, pulling me in for a kiss. I prepared for a light peck, but when I felt the wetness of a tongue, I opened my lips to deepen it, my tongue tangling with his for a moment before he pulled away.

"See you later." He winked, and then walked away, leaving me the most hated girl in the school.

And I didn't even care.

Sage and I walked out together and went our separate ways. She went to the security building for her training and I went to the arts building. As I walked, two guards trailed behind me. Quan and Brandon this time.

My mind slowly processed what just happened, the fact that Sawyer killed Vicon.

His words replayed on a loop inside my head and pinged around my soul, settling in my heart.

He's never going to hurt you again, Demi. Or anyone else.

For the past six years, I never once thought that he could be doing this on the regular. That he would hurt another girl…I assumed since that "wild animal" had murdered three of his friends for raping me, he'd have been scared off. But what if he wasn't…what if…?

The thought made me sick. I should have pushed harder for him to be arrested, I should have gone to the alpha maybe…but being banished, I had no rights.

My chest constricted as heavy emotions welled up inside of my body.

He's dead.

He couldn't hurt me or anyone else again.

Sawyer went hunting and slayed my nightmares. Tears leaked from my eyes as the reality hit me and I diverted from the open classroom door to the bathroom. Luckily, there was no one inside, because the moment I burst in the open doors I broke out in sobs. Rushing to the large bathroom stall, I opened it and slipped inside, sliding against the door to fall on my butt.

Vicon Drake stole something from me.

My virginity, my innocence, my youth, my safety, my ability to trust, everything. I'd shoved it all down because it was the only way to survive, but now that he was gone, it bubbled up to the surface, begging to be freed.

Before I could even think about it, I felt my wolf stir, and then she was walking out of my body, like a spectral ghost, becoming semisolid within seconds. It didn't really hurt anymore, it was just a tightness on my skin and then she was there. No tearing of my clothes or fur on my arms. It's like we were learning to become more and more separate. She turned and looked at me with those patient yellow eyes.

'It was me that night. I'm sorry I couldn't get the last one.' Her voice was mine but deeper, and it hit me. She was the darkest part of me, split off to help me survive. She held all of those memories of that night, the ones I blacked out. She held them for me so I didn't have to deal with them.

"Thank you," I sobbed, and reached out to her as she nestled into my open arms and I wrapped her in a hug. I might be a demon, or a split shifter, or whatever the hell these fairy tales called me, but my wolf saved me that night. As far as I was concerned, I was a fucking survivor.

I legitimately had no idea what this surprise was. My mind was still chewing on the fact that Sawyer had straight-up disappeared for three days and killed Prince Drake. Sage drove me all around campus for thirty minutes, confusing me as to what this surprise was, and then turned the car around and parked back at the dorms.

I looked at her. "Woman, what in the hell are you doing?"

She grinned. "I had to waste time while your surprise was set up in your room."

Emotion clogged my throat. She was clearly going to painstaking lengths to give me something, and that really touched me. I didn't grow up with many friends. Mostly just Raven, and so having Sage here meant the world to me. She went to get out of the car and I grabbed her arm.

She looked back at me with her beautiful red hair splayed around her shoulders and I swallowed hard.

“Thanks for being so awesome. Seriously, I couldn’t have survived the past few months without you.”

She grinned, and she looked a little like Sawyer when she smiled. “I always wanted a sister, and when you marry Sawyer, it will be close enough.”

I chuckled. “Well, he hasn’t *technically* proposed yet.”

And the very thought simultaneously had nerves crawling up my spine and excitement thrumming through my belly.

Sage looked back at me, halfway out of the car. “You know when you’re not around what he calls you to Walsh, and me, and all his guy friends? What he called you the day he ordered us to get you out of that shithole school and end your banishment?”

My stomach tightened into knots. “Wolf Girl?”

“‘My future *wife*.’” She emphasized the wife. “Hey, Sage, go get my future *wife* out of Delphi. Hey guys, I need to buy my future *wife* a camera, what is the best one? He’s never called you by your name, Demi. Not to me, or any of the guys he hangs with.”

A lightness fell over me, a pure feeling that I’d never felt before. It started deep inside of my gut and then grew upward until it feathered out of my chest and into my arms.

I’d never felt loved before. The guys at Delphi hit on me and I knew Isaac was attracted to me, but *this* feeling, feeling adored and loved and wanted, I’d never felt it in a relationship with a guy before.

With that, she left the car and beckoned for me to follow. I wiped at my eyes and scrambled after her.

"Did I mention I'm not a fan of surprises?" I ran after Sage, ducking into the dorm and down our hallway as she waved me closer.

"Hurry, we only have an hour!" she called out and checked her watch.

What in the *world*? Something was waiting for me in my room and we only had an hour to enjoy it? Was it an ice cream cake? Or an ice sculpture…or maybe—

Sage threw open the door and yelled, "Surprise!"

When I saw my mother, father, and Raven standing in my apartment, I burst into sobs.

"Those are good tears, right? I did good right?" Sage asked, frowning in confusion.

I reached out and tackle-hugged her, nearly knocking her over. "You did so good."

When I pulled back, she was grinning. "Sawyer had to beg his dad, and they can only stay for an hour."

I nodded, so overwhelmed with emotion, and she turned to leave.

"No, stay. I want you to meet them." I pulled her hand.

Her face brightened, green eyes alight. "You sure?"

I nodded. "Absolutely."

We stepped into the room and closed the door.

My mom, dad, and Raven were patiently waiting for me, standing in front of my couch. My dad was full-on crying; he was the emotional one. My mom was grinning, trying to look unemotional, but I saw the glisten in her eyes. Raven just looked around my room in wonder.

"Holy shifter balls, your dorm is amazing," she said, causing my mom to shoot her a glare and she winced. "I mean holy shifter ball-oons, this dorm is amazing."

I grinned, crashing into my bestie as she wrapped her arms around me. Her sage, frankincense, and lavender scent surrounded me; I missed that smell so damn much. That smell that said she was working all day on her spell work. "Holy crap I've missed you."

I pulled away and introduced her to Sage.

"We already know each other." Sage gave her a hug and I frowned.

Raven nodded. "She stole your phone and got my number and we've been texting to arrange this."

I grinned at Sage, unable to keep from smiling. The two of them started talking and I moved to my father, who when I hugged him, lifted me off the ground and spun me around. "I missed you so much, kiddo."

Even at twenty-one years old, he still called me kiddo and I wondered if he always would. He set me down and picked up my wrists to look at my cuff-less arms. "You're free." A tear slid from his cheek and he quickly wiped it away.

I swallowed hard. I was free, but not really able to shift in front of others because I was a split shifter. But I wasn't going to tell him that. I just nodded, smiling and giving him this moment. When I got to my mother, she was grinning ear to ear. Reaching out, she smoothed my hair like she had a hundred times. "This place suits you." She looked around my dorm. "Never thought I would be back. Lexington was my dorm too. Room four."

My eyes widened and I smiled. "That's cool."

My mom leaned into me and lowered her voice. "So tell me about Sawyer."

I couldn't help the full-fledged grin that graced my face. "He's…perfect. Protective and respectful and sweet. I didn't really expect him to be a nice guy."

My mom chuckled. "Sounds like his father. Curt was a nice guy." Something dark crossed her features and she frowned.

Then I remembered that she was banished Curt's mating year, and I suddenly found myself wondering why. She must have read my mind, because her gaze flicked to my dad, who nodded, and then she looked back at me. "Can we talk privately in your room? I need to tell you something."

The room pressed in on me, becoming smaller and smaller, and I nodded.

Holy crap. This was it, this was the moment when she was going to tell me why she got kicked out.

Breathe, just breathe.

I always secretly thought my dad murdered someone, or something really dark, to get our entire family banished from Werewolf City. Now I would hear the truth.

She stepped into my room and I shut the door behind me. She sat on the edge of my bed and patted the spot next to her. Seeing her sitting there, her long beautiful blond hair in a thick braid over one shoulder, I couldn't help but think how much we looked alike. But there was stress behind her eyes, something that aged her more than her forty-two years, but damn, she was still gorgeous.

We sat there a moment, just being in stillness, until finally my mother took my hand and faced me. "Your grandmother's land, the land I grew up on in Werewolf City, bordered the Paladin Wild Lands." My body went rigid, as I had no idea the Paladin's would factor into this story.

"The Paladins are a rival pack, absolutely hated by the alpha and expressly forbidden to have contact with," she told me.

I nodded, indicating she go on. She had no idea I already knew who the Paladins were or that I'd met one and he'd saved my life.

"But I was just a kid, I didn't know that. So at nine years old when my foot got stuck in the barn slats while I was feeding the chickens, I wailed for help but my mom was vacuuming and couldn't hear me."

I leaned closer, desperate for this story. "But another boy did. He was eleven, and he burst into the barn wearing some kind of caveman getup and holding a spear."

She smiled at the memory, and I immediately was reminded of the nice Paladin man who'd saved me and how he'd dressed so barbaric.

"I was frightened of him at first, but when he pried my leg free I gave him some fresh eggs for the trouble. Soon after that, we met at the border flags every day and exchanged gifts and told stories. He became my best friend."

Holy shit, this was *not* what I expected. Would they banish my mom for having a Paladin best friend? That's a bit wild.

I leaned forward. "What happened?"

My mom looked away, and when she turned back to me her cheeks were red. "His name was Running Spirit, but I just called him Run." She smiled at the memory. "We grew older and his body started to change. He went from a boy to a man."

Ohhh, so that's where this story is going. I braced myself.

She blushed, seemingly lost in memories.

"On my fifteenth birthday, he kissed me and I fell in love with him. He was seventeen and said he would be going away for a while. Some kind of Paladin rite. He was the son of the alpha and needed to prove himself on some type of vision quest or something. He asked me if I would wait for him and I said yes."

My heartbeat thundered in my chest and I nodded. "What happened? How long was he gone?" The story enthralled me completely.

My mom sighed. "Too long. I waited every day by the back fence for three *years* until I got my letter that Curt Hudson wanted me to attend Sterling Hill because it was his mate selection year."

Three years? Holy crap, that was too long. Did he die?

Sadness crossed her face. "I had to choose to wait for him or go follow my dream of going to college. As you know, it was free, and this would be my only chance to get this kind of education and make a better life for your grandmother and me. I grew up poor and we had a small farm, but it wasn't enough, even with the handouts from Wolf City...it was a hard life."

A tear slipped out from my eye because I'd never heard this story and I couldn't imagine having to choose between something like that. I'd never met my grandmother, but I spoke to her a few times on the phone before she passed away over a decade ago. Every picture we had of her, she wore a dirty apron and was cooking or milking a cow. Now I understood why. I guess it was a lie to think every wolf inside the city borders was rich and taken care of.

"What happened, Mom? You can tell me."

She swallowed hard and nodded. "I lied to you about not making the top twenty with Curt..."

I froze. Okay…was not expecting that. Oh Lord, please don't tell me she had an affair with Curt and Sawyer was my half-brother or some shit.

She must have read my mind, because she laughed nervously. "I never even kissed him."

All the air I'd been holding released from me in a rush, but she chewed her bottom lip. "I met your father the first day of class here. I liked him right away. Smart, funny, and cute. He kept his distance romantically because of the mating selection, but there was an undeniable chemistry there."

I smiled thinking of my mom and dad falling in love.

"We started to meet in the library late at night to study. His hand would brush mine or I'd find an excuse to touch him. We quickly realized we were falling for each other, and I had somehow made it to the top five."

Oh God, talk about awkward! "What did you do?"

Her lips puffed out as she blew air through them.

"Well, I'm not proud of this, but…on Christmas break I went home to visit my mom…and Run was waiting for me in the barn."

I gasped. "Wait? What? He was back?"

She nodded, chewing her lip in anxiety. "He was back, he was alpha, and he was *insanely* good looking."

I gulped, my heart torn at the story.

"Why was he gone so long?" I suddenly felt like I was watching a soap opera and needed to know every detail.

My mom shrugged. "We didn't do much talking..." She let that sentence linger and my eyes went wide.

"I was dating Curt, falling in love with your father, and already in love with Run. I was a mess, so confused, and when he kissed me, all of that fell away and...we made love right there in the barn for the first time." She winced.

Okay, embarrassing to hear my mom say that, but I needed to hear this story. "Wow," was all I could think of to say.

She nodded. "I guess Curt was suspicious that I was secretly dating your father, so he had me followed, and a guard caught us in the barn."

Oh shit. *Plot twist.* "Did they arrest you?"

She pulled her hand from mine and walked to the window. The curtains were closed but she stared at them and rubbed her temples.

"He was a Paladin, Demi. They killed him. Right there in front of me. Said he was trespassing and called it rape."

Bile rose in my throat. To misuse that word made anger rise up in me so strongly I felt dizzy.

"Oh, Mom, I'm so sorry." I stood and stepped closer to meet her at the window and she spun around.

"I'm not done, Demi." She held out her hand as if she didn't want me to come closer. Tears lined her eyes, but she blinked them back. I'd never seen my mom cry. Every sad movie we watched, my father cried with me but not my mom. She was the rock of the family, and seeing her eyes well up now shook me.

"I couldn't let Run go like that, let them smear his name and call him a rapist."

I nodded and she took a deep breath. "I told Curt what happened, that I'd known Run since he was eleven and that it was consensual, that it was my first time with him and that I loved him." She pressed her palms to her eyelids and came away with smudged makeup and wet cheeks. "He was so mad, so furious that I chose a Paladin over him, that he banished me right there. He said he'd fallen in love with me during the selection. I had no idea."

Holy shit...Curt must have really loved my mom... not that this was any way to treat someone you loved, but it explained the anger.

"I rushed to my dorm to pack my things," my mom said. "Wondering what I would do for food and shelter, wondering how I could live in a human world alone... when your dad showed up to my dorm." This time a sob escaped her and she clutched her chest. "He said he heard of my banishment and couldn't bear to think of me out in the human world all alone. He told me he'd fallen in love with me somewhere during those late nights in the library and asked me to marry him."

Now I was crying too. That was *so* my dad, such a sweetheart and always doing the right thing. Wow, my mom had three guys in love with her at the same time. Talk about drama.

"I told your father about Run and he said he didn't care, that he knew I would grow to love him in time and we could take it slow."

"That's so Dad," I half sobbed, and she nodded, smiling and wiping back tears.

"We took it slow, but I quickly fell in love with him. You know your father, there isn't much not to love. He provided for us while I went to community college and got my teaching degree."

I smiled, feeling lightness in my chest. This story was bad, but not as bad as I feared, and it just made me love my parents more.

"Thanks for telling me, Mom." I went to hug her and she held up a hand.

I froze, a stone sinking in my gut.

"Demi, one month into living outside of Wolf City, we found out I was pregnant." Her voice shook and I blinked back shock. What was she saying?

Her cheeks reddened. "Your father and I hadn't been intimate all the way like that yet, and so...Demi, you're half Paladin," she blurted out.

The world swam around me as dizziness took over. What? Run was... *My dad wasn't my real father?*

"No!" she growled. "Don't you do that, don't you fucking dare." She cursed for the first time ever and it scared the shit out of me. "I see what you're thinking. That man out there..." She pointed to the living room. "He pulled you from between my legs when you were born, he cut your umbilical cord, he changed every diaper, he stayed when most men would leave. *That* man is your father."

I nodded, tears slipping down my cheeks as my chest tightened. She was right of course, but I couldn't help but think of poor Run, who might have been a great father had he been given the chance. Still, it wouldn't change my feelings for my dad, who I just loved more now after hearing this story. "Dad knows?"

She nodded. "Of course, I tell him everything. Demi…I'm so sorry I didn't tell you sooner. It's such a painful story for me and it doesn't really matter. We started a family a little sooner than planned but that's it. End of discussion. You were wanted. You were conceived in love and born of love and—*oofh*."

I crashed into her, squeezing her so hard the breath rushed out of her lungs and into my ear.

"And I totally understand," I told her, my voice breaking. Her arms wrapped around me and we held each other for a long while, until we finally pulled away, wiping our eyes.

"Do I look like a raccoon?" she asked, wiping at some smudged mascara.

I grinned. "Just a little bit racoon." I reached out and wiped some more black off of her cheeks.

She sighed. "That was heavy, but I feel better."

I laughed. "I agree, we need ice cream immediately."

And with that we joined everyone else in the main

room. Sage ordered ice cream sundaes for all of us and I sat next to my dad, leaning into him so he could wrap his arm around me. When Sage was showing my mom and Raven something on the TV, I leaned in closely to my dad and whispered in his ear. "I'm so lucky you're my father. I love you so much, Dad."

He swallowed hard, a tear slipping from his eye as he pulled me in for a hug. "I love you too, kiddo. You and your mother are my whole world."

I tried not to think about Curt banishing my mom and how unfair that was. I tried not to think of the nice Paladin man who got beheaded because of me when I fell down the mountain. I really tried not to think about what Sawyer would do if he found out what I was. I just let my dad hold me, and pretended everything was going to be okay.

After seeing my parents and Raven out to a car that Quan was driving, I thanked Sage for the surprise and slipped back into my apartment. Sawyer asked me to come over after, but I couldn't; I needed to absorb the fact that I was half Paladin, that I was born of the blood of Sawyer's family's mortal enemies.

I looked down at my phone. I wanted to text him or DM him on Insta, but he wasn't big on technology and social media. His WolfDude_4 profile only existed to like and comment on my photos.

Taking a deep breath, I called him instead.

"Hey, beautiful. You coming over?" he answered and I smiled.

"Actually I'm kinda wiped out emotionally. I was just calling to see if tomorrow was okay to meet up instead."

"Are you okay?" His voice was suddenly protective and alert.

I nodded, and then remembered he couldn't see me. "Yeah. Just some heavy stuff with my mom."

"Oh," he sighed. "I thought you would like having them here. Otherwise, I never would have gotten it approved."

"No, I do. I have a really good relationship with my parents. It's just..." I really wanted to tell Sawyer, but I didn't think he could handle this and still love me, so I told a half truth. "Do you know why my mom was banished?"

His sharp intake of breath told me everything I needed to know. "Yes. She had a love affair with a Paladin during my father's selection year."

I winced. When he said it like that, it sounded bad, but hearing my mother tell the story was different. His words were true, but it wasn't my mother's fault she loved a kind man who she'd known since childhood.

"Sawyer?"

"Yeah."

"Why do you guys hate the Paladins so much?"

He was silent a moment, then he breathed into the phone long and deep. "You know that story I told you about the curse that witch put on my family one thousand years ago?"

My heart threatened to jump out of my throat. "Yes," I croaked.

Don't say it. Don't say what I think you are about to.

"Well, that woman was half Danai and half Paladin wolf, their alpha."

Fuck. The Danai were the dark witches…

"So the Paladins are…like the Ithaki? Hybrids? They have female alphas?"

I'd never heard of such a thing; my head spun. Ithaki were fey hybrids, and Paladins were wolf ones. Holy shit.

"Yes. But the witch bloodline has obviously diluted over a millennium. Should I come over? We can talk about this more." He sounded concerned.

My mind spun with all of this knowledge, but I shook my head. "No. No, I'm tired, I just want to process this and sleep."

"Okay, yeah. See you at breakfast?" He sounded hopeful.

"See you then."

When he hung up, I looked down at my hands and wondered if there was a way to see if I had any witch blood inside of me.

Obviously not. Oh my God, Sawyer would never marry me if he knew what I was...

My mind shuffled through all of this information until about one a.m. when I finally passed out from exhaustion.

CHAPTER FIFTEEN

I awoke to a blaring siren. My eyelids snapped open and my phone rang.

"Hello." I was groggy and out of it. What time was it? Why didn't the siren stop when I answered the phone?

"Stay in your dorm. Don't leave no matter what," Sawyer told me, and hung up.

What the...? It hit me then that the siren was the *vampire* attack siren.

I bolted upright and looked at the clock. Three a.m.

Rushing to my closet, I threw on jeans, and then did a ten second teeth brush and tied my hair up in a bun. Why was I getting ready? I had no idea, but if the freaking vamps were here, I wanted to be ready for anything.

Someone banged on my door and I froze. Were they coming for me again?

"Open up!" Sage yelled, and relief rolled through me.

I pulled open the door to see her gripping a samurai sword in one hand, and a gun at her hip. Throwing stars and stakes were tucked into her belt.

"Whoa. What's going on?" I backed up into the room and shut the door behind her.

Sage sighed. "They're here to arrest Sawyer."

It was like time stopped. My mouth went dry at her words. "What! Who?"

Her hands shook. "Well, I assume so. My mom just texted me that the Drakes are here investigating the murder of their son."

Oh shit, shit, shit. As much as I loved Sawyer for avenging my honor or whatever, and wiping that douchebag off the face of this earth, killing the prince of the most powerful vampire coven in the country was not smart.

"At three a.m.!" I shouted.

She shrugged. "It's day for them. Vampires, remember?"

Duh. I knew that. The vampires at Delphi had to take special pills to keep them awake in order to go to school, and then another set of pills to be able to sleep at night and adapt in the human world. Contrary to fantasy stories, they could go out in the sun, it just wasn't natural for them. Their circadian rhythm was all off.

"Where are they holding him?" I moved for the door and she reached out to stop me.

"In the registration building, but you can't go. The alpha is sending guards to keep an eye on you and I. They know we will try to interfere."

I chewed my lip. "Well, why are you armed to the teeth if we can't help?"

She paced my carpet. "I dunno. In case they attack."

I froze, a thought coming to me: "The alpha is sending guards to watch over us?"

She nodded. "My mother said to behave."

"How much time do we have before they get here?"

My wolf stirred under my skin, ready to protect Sawyer.

"Seconds. Maybe a minute. Why?"

I swallowed hard, hoping this didn't hurt our friendship in the future. "Look, I'm sorry I never told you, but...I'm a split shifter and my wolf is about to walk out of my body and separate from me. Don't freak out."

Her face screwed up like she'd sucked a lemon. "What?"

Then it happened. My wolf appeared before me, a white mist crawling off my body. Sage stumbled backward in shock.

"What the fuck!" She looked at my wolf wide-eyed as she materialized into a solid form.

"It's okay. It's my wolf. We can separate," I told her, hands out before me in an effort to calm her.

"This isn't happening." Sage closed her eyes and then opened them, shaking her head.

There was a knock at the door and my wolf tensed.

"Coming. I'm getting dressed!" I shouted, and ran for the living room window. Sage stood there in shock as I opened the window and let my wolf slink out into the dark night. "Protect Sawyer," I told her, and she nodded. We were one, but we were also two people. It was hard to explain, but one thing we agreed on was that we loved Sawyer, and he should be protected no matter what.

I shut the window and Sage was still frozen beside me. "How far apart can you go? How is this possible?"

"Tell you later. Promise." I pulled her from the window so it wouldn't look suspicious and then went to open the door.

Two giant guards I didn't recognize pushed their way into my apartment, silver stakes at their side. "There's an emergency on campus, Miss Calloway," the one with a shaved head said. "We need to make sure you're safe." He slipped into my room and checked the bathroom and closet. Seemingly checking for vampires.

"I'm keeping her safe," Sage growled, gripping the sword in her hands.

I zoned out of what they were saying and concentrated on my wolf. She was running in the shadows, through the quad and toward the admin building where I'd gone the first day. The campus was crawling with security, but my wolf was agile and quiet; she moved behind bushes and through shadows. Sage spoke with the security guards while I walked toward my bedroom.

"I'm just going to lie down. It's late and I'm tired." My voice trailed off as I kept my attention with my wolf.

"Leave the door open," one of the guards said.

"I'm gonna lie down too." Sage fake yawned. "*So* tired."

She followed me into my bedroom.

I sat on the bed and lay on the pillow, keeping my sight with my wolf, who had just reached the closed doors of the admin building. The lights were on inside, so there must be people in there. There were two guards there; my wolf stood in the bushes just to the right of them. Damn. I was kind of hoping for a door left open like in the movies.

No such luck.

"They said murder charges," one of the guards said and I grew still.

"That's kind of badass," the other said. "The vampires have been messing with us for too long. Sawyer will be a good alpha. He won't take their shit like his father."

The first guard scoffed. "You can't be an alpha from Magic City Jail, bro."

"Whatever."

Magic City Jail?

Shit. I knew there was a city for each race, and as a

whole they were all a part of Magic City but...I didn't know there was a jail.

Backtracking, I slipped along the side of the building, in the dark, trying not to crunch on leaves or make any noise to alert the guards.

Sage pulled me from my wolf's reality. "Can you like...feel her still, or talk to her?"

I nodded. "She's at the building, looking for Sawyer."

"Holy shit," Sage breathed. "Tell me what happens."

I nodded again and focused back on my wolf.

What was she doing? She had gotten really close to one of the dark tinted windows, so close her nose was fogging it. I felt a tug at my navel like she was pulling something from me. Before I could try to figure it out, she went all translucent like she did before she jumped back in my body and...*walked through* the glass door, coming out on the other side in an empty conference room.

"Holy shit," I breathed.

"What's wrong?" Sage gripped my hand, but I kept my eyes closed, because it was the only way I knew how to concentrate.

"Nothing. I mean...my wolf just walked through a wall but nothing."

"That's *not* normal," Sage whispered, and I didn't really have anything to say to that, because she was right. It wasn't.

My wolf solidified and then peered out into the

hallway. Immediately voices carried to her. She slinked down the hallway to get closer to them.

"We have security footage showing two wolves, gray and black, crossing the south side of our border two days ago," a male voice said as my wolf listened on.

"And now my son is dead!" a woman spat.

My wolf crept closer, standing just beyond the doorway.

"Half of our wolves are gray or black, it's the most common coloring." I recognized the alpha's voice.

"And your *son* happens to be a gray wolf, does he not?" the woman hissed. I recognized her voice, it was Vicon's mother, the queen of all the vampires in Vampire City.

"Are you saying you think *my* son killed yours?" It was the first time I'd ever heard Sawyer's mom speak in a threatening or strong tone; she was always so soft-spoken and polite.

"Well, if he didn't, then why *the hell* is he grinning like an idiot right now?" Queen Drake spat.

"Because I hate your kind." Sawyer's voice could cut glass and my wolf went very still.

"And I want you *off* our land. Now."

Silence fell over the room and my heart leapt into my throat as my wolf stepped inside.

'No!' I hissed to her mentally, *'You'll be seen!'*

Wait...why was no one looking at me? My wolf walked right up to the table and I was shocked to see a lot more people there than I'd thought. Sawyer, his mom, Curt, and then Vicon's parents, King and Queen Drake. I knew them from when my parents made the complaint. I'd met them for all of five minutes, but they weren't two people you'd forget. There were also two men in suits, one sitting on each side...they looked like lawyers. The person at the head of the table shocked me the most.

Prime Minister Locke. Were the light fey like Switzerland in these situations? Maybe they were a neutral third party.

"We want a full investigation, Curt." Vicon's dad slammed his flat palm on the table and glared at the alpha.

Holy shit, he looked so much like Vicon it made the hair on my wolf stand up. His dark hair was slicked over to one side, and it looked wet but probably just had a shitload of gel in it. He wore a crisp black satin suit with a black shirt and black tie. All of this was in stark contrast to his paper white skin.

Sawyer suddenly turned his head, very slowly, and looked right at me, eyes widening a little, before looking away quickly. Vicon's mother did the same, following Sawyer's gaze, but seemed to look past my wolf, and then away like she couldn't see me.

What the hell?

"Of course. We will conduct an internal investigation and hand over our report to you when it's complete."

Curt interlaced his fingers and set them on the table, giving the vampires a cold hard glare.

Sawyer dropped his hand underneath the table and wiggled his fingers, as if beckoning my wolf. She trotted over to him and he sank his fingers into my fur.

"Internal investigation?" Queen Drake barked in laughter. "The prince of Vampire City was brutally *murdered*. We have DNA wolf hair from the scene that we will be crosschecking with *all* of your wolves."

Mr. Hudson went very still then, his eyes flashing yellow as he stood. "Over. My. Dead. Fucking. Body," he growled.

Whoa. Our normally reserved alpha had finally lost his shit.

King Drake stood, glaring him down. "That can be arranged."

The table erupted into shouts and the prime minister clapped loudly. "That's enough!" he screamed, causing everyone to fall quiet.

Prime Minister Locke looked at the Drakes. "Your vampires have been sticking their noses where they don't belong lately. The wolves have had *two* attacks on campus—"

King Drake tipped his chin up. "Without our knowledge!"

Yeah, right.

Locke shrugged. "Nevertheless, you are not wholly innocent in all of this."

"So my son deserves to be murdered?" Queen Drake slammed her fist on the table. "I want some fucking justice!"

Locke looked to her and nodded. "Absolutely. So we will let the wolves conduct their internal investigation and bring forth the wolf or wolves responsible, but asking for an entire DNA database of their pack is unreasonable."

Queen Drake hissed, looking feral, but sat down.

Curt gave a smug smile to his wife and then looked at Locke. "Thank you for mediating. I think it's time our *guests* left. The sun is coming up soon after all. They must be very tired."

The Drakes narrowed their eyes at the alpha and he and his wife stood. Their useless lawyer who hadn't spoken the entire time glared at Prime Minister Locke. "We will be filing a petition with the Magical Creatures Council to have the DNA sample crosschecked with the wolves brought forward from their *internal investigation.*" He patted his maroon leather briefcase to indicate the sample was inside.

Locke nodded. "Sounds like a reasonable request."

Sawyer stiffened slightly, his fingers still in my fur. Was that his DNA hair sample in there? Obviously…

As the vampires reached the door, Sawyer spoke: "What's the consequence in Vampire City for brutal rape?"

My wolf froze at the same time King and Queen Drake did. The entire room froze at that actually.

Queen Drake's voice was like a loaded weapon. "Why do you ask?"

Sawyer shrugged carelessly. "Just curious."

Awkward silence descended on the room as King Drake's jaw clenched. "*If* found convicted, brutal rape carries a death sentence in our coven."

Sawyer grinned, the cockiest fucking grin I'd ever seen, and my wolf practically purred. The queen lunged for Sawyer, darting halfway across the room, but the lawyer was faster. He zipped in front of her, grasping her by the shoulders.

"Save it for the courtroom," he hissed.

She looked over the lawyer's shoulder and pinned a feral gaze at Sawyer. "I can't *wait* until you become alpha next year." Her grin was practically as scornful as Sawyer's, and a stone sank in my gut. It was a promise. A promise of revenge?

"I'll escort you out." Prime Minister Locke cleared his throat and left the room with them.

The wolf lawyer stood then, looking at the open door for a moment, until he was sure it was clear. "A witch owes me a favor..." His voice was barely a whisper. "I'll see if she can change Sawyer's DNA for a while. If not, we need to break in and steal that briefcase."

Holy shit, *okay*, so everyone at this table knew Sawyer was guilty.

"Thank you, Phineas." Mrs. Hudson stood and

escorted him out, leaving Sawyer and his father staring each other down.

Curt's nostril flared. "You need to learn to curb your anger, son."

Sawyer barked out a laugh. "I love you, Father, but with all due respect, you're not angry enough."

Curt stood, veins flaring in his neck. "You think I don't want to wipe every bloodsucker off the face of the earth? They're a constant thorn in my side, but if I acted on every instigation, we'd be at war."

Sawyer let go of my fur and stood, leaning into his father as alpha power spread throughout the room, becoming like a heavy blanket. "*Instigation?* That motherfucker raped her. Pinned her down with three of his friends and *stole* her virginity."

Curt quickly looked down at the table, avoiding his son's gaze in a clear show of submission that nearly knocked my wolf backward.

Sawyer was much more dominant than his father, that was very clear.

"You can't go murdering every person that—"

"What if it was Sage?" Sawyer's voice was barely human. "What if that blood bag had raped Sage?" Sawyer asked his father.

Curt's eyes flashed yellow. "I'd tear him limb from limb," Curt growled, fur rising on his neck.

Sawyer nodded, and Curt shook his head at his son. "You *really* love her."

My heart beat wildly in both my wolf and my human body.

"I do," Sawyer said boldly.

His father nodded, looking a bit sad. "Let's hope for all of our sakes that she's not like her mother and that she feels the same."

Ouch. I would be pissed at that comment if I didn't see a painful memory cross his face. He really had loved my mom…that was so clear, and because of the curse he had to marry someone who loved him. Mrs. Hudson. I felt sad now wondering if he'd grown to love her, or if he just respected her.

I guess it wasn't my business.

"Good night, son." Curt turned and left the room, letting the door close behind him.

When he was gone, Sawyer looked down at me with a lopsided grin. "When did you get the power of invisibility?"

My wolf snuggled into his hand and Sawyer shook his head in amazement, kneeling down to pet my ears. "I can't really fully see you, you look like a ghost to me. But I could sense you. The moment you walked in, I knew."

My wolf nuzzled into him, and he pulled my face up to look up at his. "Send Demi to my apartment. I need to see her," he said, then he leaned down and kissed the top of my snout.

With a nod, my wolf took off down the hallway,

through the glass wall, and then headed back to the dorm.

"All right, ladies," the two guards in my dorm shouted, shaking Sage and I from our trance. "The threat is gone, you can go back to sleep."

We thanked them and they left, and then Sage yanked on my arm. "Tell me everything. What the fuck, Demi?"

I sighed. "You know how I told you about my... attack?" I tried not to use the "r" word too much. People didn't like the word rape, that's why a child rapist was called a pedophile. It softened the blow.

She nodded.

"Well..." My voice shook. "With the cuffs on...I couldn't shift and protect myself so my wolf...split."

Her hands came to her face, grasping the edges of her mouth. "Ohmygod, I'm so sorry." She reached out and held my hands.

I nodded, thanking her, and told her how I only just discovered it the night I shifted for the first time with Sawyer. I didn't yet tell her I was half Paladin, I was still processing that one. But I told her everything I'd just overheard in the meeting room.

Sage looked hopeful. "That's good. If the witch can change Sawyer's DNA, then it won't even go to trial."

"And if she can't?" My voice cracked. Trial? I wondered if there was like a magical court system or something.

Before either of us could remark on that, my wolf

was back, trotting into the room like it was no big deal. She must have walked through the glass window again.

Weird. Would never get used to that one.

"That was wild. What other powers do you have?" I asked my wolf and reached out a hand to her. She gave me a lopsided grin and then went semitransparent, joining our bodies into one.

"That's…I'm sorry, girl, but that's some *freaky* shit." Sage laughed and I joined her. It was. I wasn't going to deny that.

I popped to my feet and smoothed my hair. It was four a.m. and Sawyer wanted to see me. Was that considered a booty call?

I certainly hoped so.

Sage had a devilish grin. "Where you going?"

"To see Sawyer." I winked.

Sage smiled, but then her face faltered. "Hey, Demi? Don't break him. He's fragile, okay?"

My brow furrowed at that. If anyone was going to get hurt or broken, it was *definitely* me. And Sawyer wasn't someone I would call fragile, but I nodded anyway to assure her. She was just protecting her cousin.

"Promise," I told her, wondering what would make her say that. She and Sawyer seemed to be close, and I wondered now what he'd told her about me.

I'd always been told I was a bit aloof emotionally and hard to read. Sometimes I forgot that I came across like that. Sawyer knew how much I cared about him, right?

Now I wasn't so sure.

The moment I stepped out into the hallway of my dorm, Eugene was waiting for me. "Sawyer is expecting you," he said.

A short five-minute golf cart ride across campus later and I was at Sawyer's front door.

It was late, I was tired, but I couldn't stop replaying the things he said to his father about me in my head. The way he'd stuck up for me. No one had ever done that for me before, not even my parents. After the attack, their hands were tied. They'd filed the complaint, but they were two poor banished wolves living out in the human world. Sawyer had just stared down his father, the alpha of all of Wolf City, and told him that he should be angrier about what happened to me.

My chest tightened with emotion and I knocked softly on the door. When he pulled it back, eyes roaming over my face, checking for any signs of distress, something burst open inside of me.

I loved him. I really fucking loved him. He was a catch, not just because he was rich or the future alpha or any of that shit. He was sweet and sexy and he fought for me. He'd killed for me. Twice.

"I'm in love with you!" I blurted out, causing a grin to pull at his lips as Eugene took this moment to back up and give us privacy. "I mean, I'm not good with this fuzzy feelings shit, but I'm so fucking in love with you it hurts." I grabbed my chest and he stepped out into the doorway and grasped the sides of my face. Looking down at me with searing blue eyes, he smiled, showing me his chin butt in all its glory.

"Can I kiss you?" he asked, looking at my lips.

I looked at him through a half-lidded gaze and started to push him back into his apartment with my hips, pressing my pelvis into him until we were inside, then I shut the door behind me. Leaning forward, I trailed my tongue along his salty neck and then whispered in his ear. "Make love to me, Sawyer."

It was like he was made of combustible materials and I'd just lit him on fire. His skin flared with heat as his warm lips crashed to mine in a hungry kiss that confirmed every feeling I had.

I was made for him.

He was made for me.

And fuck anyone who tried to stand in my way.

His tongue slipped into my mouth and I moaned as he swallowed my sounds. I kissed him with a feverish urgency as heat built up, threatening to burst me from the inside out. Remembering what he'd said before about letting me lead, I started to walk backward into his bedroom. His hand snaked up my shirt but stayed just under my bra, until I reached up and pushed it higher, giving him permission. When he cupped my breast, pressure exploded between my legs, causing me to growl as I pushed him backward on the bed.

He fell onto the crisp white sheets, while I stayed standing.

Reaching down to grasp the edges of my shirt, I pulled it up over my head, watching his eyes rake over me with satisfaction. He did the same, one-handed, revealing a perfect chest and abs. Unbuttoning my shorts, I let them fall to the floor as he mimicked my movements, taking his shorts off and matching me.

He lay there, in his boxers, on his back but propped up on his elbows just watching me, waiting. I had all of the control and that was sexy as hell. In one move I slipped off my bra and his eyes went yellow. Leaning forward, I crawled up his body, slowly, brushing my breasts against his stomach and tracing my nipples up his abs.

"Fuck, Demi..." he groaned, causing a satisfied grin to pull at my lips.

When I reached him, I took one of his hands and placed it on my left breast, then I leaned down slowly and took his bottom lip into my mouth. His hardness grew beneath me as I grabbed for his other hand and slipped it under my panties, between my legs.

We both moaned at the same time.

His tongue slipped into my mouth, gliding with mine as need built up inside of me.

I needed Sawyer like I've never needed a man before. One of his fingers slipped inside of me and a low satisfying groan ripped from my throat.

"Is this okay?" he asked, breathy in my ear.

I swallowed hard. "Yes." I panted as I moved my hips harder into his hand.

I pulled my mouth away from him and arched my back as he came up to take my nipple into his mouth and suck. Something unfurled inside of me as I reached between us and grabbed his hardness, stroking.

"Demi..." he groaned.

His hand came down on my lower back, and in one swift move he flipped me underneath him, with him on top of me.

"Is this okay?" he asked.

I nodded as his fingers continued to move inside of me.

"Condom?" My breaths were coming out in short gasps as he fiddled with the nightstand beside his bed. I needed to be closer to him, to come together as one. He tore the condom wrapper off with his teeth and then put it on, the entire time keeping his blue eyes locked on mine.

"Are you sure?" he asked.

I'd never been more sure about anything. From the day I'd first met him, I just had a feeling he would be special to me, something I didn't even want to admit to myself at the time.

"Absolutely."

With that, he peeled off my underwear, kissing up my thigh as he came back up, giving one lick right between my legs that nearly sent me over the edge.

He growled in satisfaction and I grasped the bedsheets as a pulsing heat throbbed between my legs. Then he was inside of me.

I cried out as pleasure filtered throughout my body with each rock of his hips. Heat, pressure, and pure fucking pleasure danced across my skin in equal measure. His lips landed on my neck, kissing as his fingers went between us, massaging my most sensitive spot.

"Is this okay?" Sawyer whispered in my ear.

"Don't stop," I managed to gasp. Everything about this was okay. The time I had sex with Isaac, it wasn't like this. Nothing I'd ever had was like this.

A dull vibration started to rattle my chest as Sawyer moved his fingers faster, pumped his hips harder. I threw my head back onto the bed and he kissed my neck before dragging his tongue along my collarbone.

Oh dear God, I was going to explode.

'I love you,' he breathed.

'I love you too,' I moaned, and then my head jerked back as I realized we'd just spoken in each other's mind.

His eyes were wide in shock as the dull vibration grew stronger, until I felt his emotions bleed into me, filling me almost as if I were tapping into my wolf's emotions.

"Do you feel that?" he asked.

I nodded, gasping as he continued rocking over me. "What is it?"

He grasped one side of my face with his free hand and

rested his forehead on mine as feelings of pure adoration rocked through me.

He adored me. He adored everything about me. My goofy shirts, my laugh, my love for photography.

"We're imprinting," he huffed, as an orgasm rocked my body.

"We're wh—?" I didn't have time to ask what that was or what it meant, because waves of bliss crashed into me as I raked my nails down his back, crying out. A bright white light emanated from my chest and then from his, meeting in the air between us and becoming a ball of blinding light.

Images flashed into my mind. They were of me…but from Sawyer's point of view. Me running out of the hall at Delphi, howling at the sky as my wolf tried to break free. Me taking pictures across campus and Sawyer watching while talking to his friends. Images of the first time I shifted and how he'd helped my wolf. Feelings of arousal, possession, love, fear, all rocked through me as I tried to make sense of what was happening.

Sawyer shuddered over me, groaning in pleasure as our bodies tightened around each other, muscles clenching as our pleasure reached a crescendo. Pulses of pleasure and magic mixed together as we both panted, and the light became so bright I had to close my eyes. Then it flared brightly and was gone as quickly as it had come.

I popped my eyes open. Sawyer climbed off of me and lay next to me, breathless.

I tried to catch my own breath, looking up at the ceiling and trying to figure out what to say.

"What the *hell* was that?" I finally asked, and then busted out laughing. He started to laugh as well, and pretty soon we were both full-on snort giggling.

Once the reality hit, that we'd just...imprinted,...my laughter died in my throat and I propped up on an elbow. "Sawyer, what's imprinting? What was that light?"

I remembered it from the first time we'd kissed. I thought it had to do with my split shifting and what the book said about being able to feed on my powers...but maybe not.

He rolled over and sighed, tucking a lock of hair behind my ear. "Did your parents ever tell you about true mates? Not just the mates we choose and marry, but the ones destined by fate?"

My mouth went dry as I shook my head.

"Demi, from the day I saw you at Delphi, I knew you were my true mate."

My heart hammered in my throat.

Were true mates like soulmates?

"I felt it too. I mean, I didn't know what it was but..." I let that sentence linger. "What is imprinting? That white light?"

He looked at me plainly, hard to read. "I don't really know. I mean, I've heard of it as a special bond between...Paladin wolves. It's a magic thing between true mates."

Oh fuck.

I wasn't calm enough to hide my response; my eyes widened and I chewed my lip as I fought for words. But Sawyer just looked...acceptingly...at me. "It's okay, Demi. I know."

I frowned. "You...know...what?"

Please don't say that I'm a Paladin.

"That you're part Paladin."

Shit. I sat upright and covered my breasts. "What? I mean, That's a big problem...right?" He stood at the end of the bed and tossed me a shirt, then walked into the bathroom and emerged a few moments later in basketball shorts.

Sitting next to me, he pulled me onto his lap. "That book page I showed you about what you are...it said the split shifting only happens with Paladins. Then I looked up why your parents were banished and found out what your mom did...I put two and two together," he confessed. "I've known for a while."

Ahhh, well, that was smart of him, and shitty for me. "You should have told me sooner." I hugged my arms and he pulled the blanket around us.

"Sorry, I was still trying to figure it all out." He tucked me tighter into his body, his warmth pressing against me. "Look, it doesn't matter to me what you are or who you are. I love you, Demi, all of you."

"So is imprinting in that book you have?" I asked.

He chuckled. "No, that comes from stories my great

grandmother told me as a child." I leaned into him, looking up at him as he smiled down on me. "It can only happen with true mates she told me, and it's a Paladin thing."

"What does imprinting mean?"

"Imprinted true mates can speak into each other's minds no matter the distance," he told me.

I shrugged. "Kinda handy."

'*Testing, testing.*' I tried.

His chin butt puckered as he grinned.

'*One, two, three...*'

Whoa, that's wild. "What else?" I couldn't help the smile that lit up my face.

He swallowed hard, reaching out to stroke my cheek. "They can feel each other's feelings. Sense things."

His fingers trailed down my neck and I shivered as they stroked the top of my breasts.

"What else?"

He shrugged. "That's all I remember. I was young when she died."

He lay back on his pillow and looked up at the ceiling as I snuggled in beside him, feeling completely at home in his arms.

"True mates, huh?" I looked up at him.

He grinned. "Can't argue with fate."

A smile tugged at my lips. "No, we can't."

I lay there on his chest, listening to the rise and fall of his breath as the weight of sleep pulled at me.

"In an endless garden of flowers, I will always pick you," Sawyer whispered in my ear and my eyelids fluttered.

"Who said that?" I muttered, my eyelids unable to stay open.

"A.J. Lawless."

I grinned, thinking of how true I wanted that statement to be. Even though Sawyer said he was picking me early at the selection ceremony, I would still be nervous until it was a done deal. I wanted to be with him, and having all of these other girls after my man was making me stabby.

CHAPTER SIXTEEN

"How do you feel?" Sage asked me as she appraised the brand-new deep blue gown Sawyer had sent over for me.

"Nervous as hell." I gulped, clutching her hand as our limo driver drove us to the lakeside country club where Sawyer was going to tell the entire selection of girls and their parents that he'd chosen me early.

I'd spent every night this week at Sawyer's, and the mind talking thing was coming in really handy.

'I feel like I'm going to puke,' I told him as the limo pulled up to the country club entrance.

'Not too late to back out,' he jived playfully in my head.

'I mean, I've only known you a few months and we are talking about marriage here. This is forever.'

'I was kidding.' His voice in my head was unsure. *'Are you really having second thoughts?'*

I laughed and Sage rolled her eyes, fully sick of the imprinting talking thing by now.

'No, I'm fucking with you. I can't wait to be your wifey. Hashtag True Mates.'

I could feel relief rush through him. *'I mean, I know we're young, and we can totally wait a few years to have kids—'*

'Sawyer, I want to be your wife,' I assured him. He hadn't technically asked yet, and there was no bling on my finger, but I gathered that this had to happen first before that could. There seemed to be a protocol with all of these events and I'm sure it was in the bylaws if I took the time to read them. On my to-do list. Really.

The limo came to a stop and the door opened. Sawyer was standing there with his arm out. "Good, because I wasn't taking no for an answer."

I grinned, stepping out and then leaning forward to kiss him. He pulled back and appraised me. "Damn, woman."

"I know, I look amazing." Sage popped her head up beside me and did a twirl.

Sawyer grinned at her and nodded. "That you do, cousin, but I was speaking about my future wife."

Sage grinned and looked at me. "See. Told you he calls you that."

I'd never seen Sawyer look happier. There was a lightness to him. His brokenness was gone, and I liked to think I had a small part to play in that.

"Sawyer!" an older woman shrieked and he winced.

It was Meredith's mom. "All right, I'll meet you ladies inside. I…gotta deal with this," he told us, swooping in to kiss my cheek.

Sage and I linked arms and walked into the building as I peered over my shoulder at Sawyer talking to Meredith and her mother. Meredith lifted onto her tiptoes and kissed his cheek, causing my wolf to growl.

Sage noticed. "It's nothing. He'll let her down privately before she can hear it publicly in front of everyone. Sawyer is a gentleman like that."

I still didn't like it, and Meredith must not have either, because she shot me a death glare before I could turn back around to face forward.

All thoughts of Meredith were temporarily washed from my mind when we stepped into the space.

"Good evening, ladies," Roland greeted us. I smiled at Sawyer's butler, whom I remembered meeting from the boat.

"Hello, Roland, good to see you."

He gave us both a smile and we entered the room.

"Oh wow," I breathed, taking in the giant crystal chandelier that hung from the middle of the large ballroom. From that, small, white twinkling string lights branched out to the corners of the room, dripping down the walls. Each chair was covered in silk satin, and the center of the tables held a stunning floral display. If this was just an announcement, I hated to think of how extravagant the wedding would be. I recognized the other girls, and that not just the top twenty were here but all fifty. It must be customary to invite everyone back once you'd chosen your mate.

"You bitch!" a familiar female called from behind me and I froze.

Turning, I saw a red-faced Meredith coming right for me.

Okay, so letting her down gently clearly hadn't worked.

Sage stepped in front of me to cut her off. "Go out on the patio. I got this," Sage told me and put her hands out to Meredith. "Don't make a scene," I heard her saying as I spun and beelined it for the balcony.

Shit.

I mean, this was *Werewolf Bachelor*, but I was hoping for a drama-free night. I really wished I'd had time to chug some champagne or something to take the edge off. The cool evening air blew past me as I stepped out onto the balcony. Taking in a few lungfuls, I tried to calm my nerves.

"There you are," Sawyer's voice called from behind me and I spun.

"I'm guessing that didn't go well?" I nodded inside, indicating to Meredith.

He smiled, ignoring my comment. "I missed you."

Okay, I just saw him like thirty seconds ago, but... "I missed you too."

He wrapped his arms around my waist and leaned down to kiss me as I threw my arms up around his neck. His lips came down on mine in a hard, aggressive way that I didn't expect. His tongue pried its way into my mouth in a hungry and rushed kiss that wasn't like him.

"What the fuck!" Sawyer screamed as alarm bells went off in my head.

How can he be screaming *while* he's kissing me? He pulled away from me and I looked up into the eyes of a man I'd never seen before.

Light blond ashy hair, hard brown eyes and a chiseled jaw.

My hands went to my mouth as shock ripped through me.

What the hell was happening? Confusion seeped into me as the brown-eyed dude grinned at me and then looked back at Sawyer. Meredith and Sage stood just behind Sawyer, watching me, both with open mouths.

Fuck.

Sawyer lunged for the guy, but he leapt over the patio railing and took off running, leaving me with my hands over my mouth and my heart beating frantically in my chest.

"Demi," Sawyer's voice held so much anger. "Who the fuck was that?" I noticed he was wearing a weird necklace he didn't have on before. It was a blue pendant on a thick chain, not his style...

My hands shook as I pulled them away from my face. "I dunno...I thought it was...*you*."

He scoffed. "You *fucking* played me!" The hurt in his voice gutted me.

"No I didn't! I'm...confused. I thought it was *you*." My fingers went to my lips again as I tried to think of a logical reason for what just happened. "Maybe I was drugged."

He frowned, suddenly looking concerned. "Do you feel drugged?"

I shook my head. "No, but—"

"Did anyone give you anything to eat or drink here?" he pressed.

"No."

"Then why the *fuck* was some random dude's tongue just down your throat!" he yelled as people in the room started to gather behind him and stare. This wasn't like him, he wasn't mean, not to me, not ever.

Tears lined my eyelids. "I...I don't know."

Anger washed over his features, before morphing into pain. "I...trusted you...with everything. Is this why you were having second thoughts on the way over? Oh my God, I feel sick."

He turned to leave and I clung to his jacket. "Sawyer, wait! I'll figure out what this was, it must have been magic—"

"No." He looked back at me with stone cold fury. "*This* was a mistake! I love you but that doesn't *mean* anything."

He lowered his head to look down at me. *'I have to look out for my family now and what's best for them. It doesn't matter that I love you. The curse only breaks if you love me back. I'm sorry, Demi. I can't risk their lives on a girl who just made out with some random dude at what was supposed to be our engagement party.'*

He jerked out of my grasp and burst through the crowd, going inside. It was like he'd smacked me in the face. Each word slammed into me like hot coals being thrown at my skin.

'Sawyer, don't do this. I love you! This was magic or something. I didn't know what I was doing!' Desperation took hold of me. *'What about the imprint? True mates?'*

I could feel his anguish through our bond, like a hurricane of emotions slamming into me with gale force winds. *'I want to believe you but...I can't. That was clearly Paladin magic and I don't want anything to do with it.'*

Pain ripped open inside of me, fresh and hot as my wolf and I felt the full brunt of his rejection. When he turned the corner, I caught a glimpse of Meredith. She was waiting for him, all sad and dopey eyed. He pulled her into a hug and my wolf reared to the surface, trying to break out and howl in misery, but I pushed her down. When Meredith looked over his shoulder at me, she was grinning.

This can't be happening.

"Miss Calloway, I'm here to escort you back to

your dorm room," Eugene said behind me in a cold and unforgiving voice. He'd walked up behind the patio and was waiting on the other side to kick me out of my own engagement party.

Fuck.

Sawyer's voice filtered out onto the balcony from inside the speakers in the room: "Hello, everyone, and thank you for coming. I've called you all here because I've made my decision early. I know who I'm meant to be with, who loves me more than anything, who has been by my side for years..."

It was like someone reached down my throat and squeezed my heart.

'Don't. She doesn't love you. Please. This was an accident,' I warned him. His entire family would die if he married Meredith. That, I was sure of.

His cold blue eyes met my gaze through the glass window, and instead of seeing the anger I expected, I just saw more broken pieces, pieces *I* broke. Pieces I promised Sage I wouldn't.

"Meredith Pepper is my future wife and mate."

The crowd erupted into applause as my heart was ripped out of my throat and a sob escaped me. I'd lost him. Lost the one guy who ever fought for me. The only guy I'd ever really trusted when trust in men was in such short supply.

Without waiting for Eugene, I leapt over the balcony, landing on my feet, and took off running. I couldn't help the soul-crushing howl that tore from my throat as my wolf and I mourned the loss of the love of our life.

My feet pounded against the black asphalt as I ran down the road and back to campus, grateful I'd worn my trusty white Converse. I needed to get out of here, like out of campus, out of Wolf City, out of fucking *here*. When I made it back to my room ten minutes later, chest heaving, tears streaking down my face, I picked up the camera Sawyer had given me. He'd replaced my broken one from my waterfall accident. Grasping it tightly in my hands, I threw it against the wall, smashing it to pieces as I screamed in agony.

Some of the paintings on the walls rattled and I wondered if it was an earthquake until I looked outside and didn't see any shaking trees.

It's me.

I'm going to die. This heartbreak is so painful I might actually die from it.

Running into my bedroom, I shoved a few belongings into a backpack and changed quickly into jeans and my Converse shoes before slipping out the open window. How could he not believe me? I know it was wild, but I'd thought that guy was him. He looked and sounded *just* like him. It had to be some kind of magic or something, although in all my time with the witches of Delphi, I'd never heard of a spell that powerful. Changing eye color or hair color sure, but...he'd looked *just* like him. Sounded just like him.

It *was* him. But it wasn't...and now everything was fucked up.

I ran through the trees that lined the campus, unsure where I wanted to go and hating that I was tethered to Sawyer still through our imprint. I could feel his anger, his hurt, his rightness in choosing Meredith, and it cut into me like glass. Night fell over Sterling Hill Academy as I ran harder, the moon lighting my path. I needed to go home. I needed my mom. I needed some alcohol to numb this pain. The problem was I didn't even know where the Magic Lands were. I'd been blindfolded on my way in, and my parents never spoke of it, just said they were "nearby." I could still be in Washington state or Idaho for all I knew. Or another freaking world.

Before I could decide how I would get out of here, a blur stepped in front of me, causing an alarmed gasp to rip from my throat as I skidded to a stop. Something bit my wrists and I whimpered when I realized they were cuffs. A half dozen vampires stood before me, all of them holding guns, right at my chest.

"We need you to come with us, dear." It was the vampire woman from before, the one who attacked us in Sawyer's apartment. Her long, glossy black hair fell in soft waves around her shoulders. It was in such stark contrast to the ugly look on her face.

My heart beat frantically in my rib cage as my mind tried to calculate what to do. Without my wolf, or my powers, I was pretty useless.

'Sawyer, there are six vampires at the southeast woods off campus. They've got me—' Pain laced up the cuffs as they sensed my mental talking with Sawyer as magic and electrocuted me.

'That's pretty pathetic,' Sawyer said in my head, and a tear rolled down my cheek. *'It's over, Demi. Just... leave me alone. You're just like your mother.'*

His words crashed into me, ripping what might have been left of my heart into a thousand pieces...and then that fucking necklace flashed into my mind. Meredith. Did she give it to him outside when he spoke to her and her mom? Was he spelled too?

Realizing Sawyer was a lost cause, I turned to run, a scream ripping from my throat, before cutting off mid-yell as something cracked the back of my head and everything went black.

AUTHOR NOTE

If you loved this book please take the time to review it as that can help authors reach new readers. I did some cool things for this release including making real Instagram profiles for Demi and Sawyer, so go on Insta and check them out! (Be sure to read the comments under the photos.)

Demi: @WolfGirl_4

Sawyer: @WolfDude_4

Also I made some really fun merch like T-shirts and sweaters from Demi's fun collection of shirts. You can check them out here:

teespring.com/stores/wolf-girl-2

Please join my Wolf Pack on Facebook as I often reveal covers and secret bookish things in there as well as doing giveaways.

Also sign up for my Newsletter so you don't miss a New Release. I don't spam and you can leave anytime. leiastone.com/newsletter/

ACKNOWLEDGMENTS

A huge thank-you to my editors at Bloom. Christa, Gretchen, and Kylie, you made this baby shine! And to my agents, Flavia and Meire, for always believing in my work. It truly takes a village to get every single book into readers' hands. I have to send out a huge thank-you my readers for buying my books and turning this passion into a career that supports my family. I'm literally living my dream. Thank you to my amazing and supportive family for sharing me with my characters. And lastly, thank you to God for this truly remarkable gift you have given me.

ABOUT THE AUTHOR

Leia Stone is the *USA Today* bestselling author of multiple bestselling series, including Matefinder, Wolf Girl, The Gilded City, Fallen Academy, and Kings of Avalier. She's sold over three million books, and her Fallen Academy series has been optioned for film. Her novels have been translated into multiple languages and she even dabbles in script writing.

Leia writes urban fantasy and paranormal romance with sassy kick-butt heroines and irresistible love interests. She lives in Spokane, Washington, with her husband and two children.

Instagram: @leiastoneauthor
TikTok: @leiastone
Facebook: leia.stone
Website: www.LeiaStone.com